ONE-HANDED CATCH

MJ AUCH

SQUARE
FISH

Henry Holt and Company

SQUARE
FISH

An Imprint of Macmillan

Square Fish and the Square Fish logo are trademarks of Macmillan and
are used by Henry Holt and Company under license from Macmillan.

Library of Congress Cataloging-in-Publication Data
Auch, Mary Jane.
One-handed catch / MJ Auch.
p.   cm.
Summary: After losing his hand in an accident in his father's butcher shop in
1946, sixth-grader Norman uses hard work and humor to learn to live with his
disability and to succeed at baseball, art, and other activities.
ISBN-13: 978-0-312-58002-5
ISBN-10: 0-312-58002-9
[1. Amputees—Fiction.   2. Self-reliance—Fiction.   3. People with disabilities—
Fiction.   4. Family life—Fiction.   5. New York (State)—History—20th century—
Fiction.]   I. Title.
PZ7.A898One 2006   [Fic]—dc22   2006000370

Originally published in the United States by Henry Holt and Company
Square Fish logo designed by Filomena Tuosto
Designed by Laurent Linn
10   9   8   7   6   5   4   3   2   1
www.squarefishbooks.com

*This book is dedicated
to my dear husband and collaborator,
Herm Auch.*

Herm Auch, at twelve years old.

ONE-HANDED CATCH

Chapter 1

"Hey, Norm, you gotta see this."

My best friend, Leon, had his face pressed up to the screen door of our family meat market. I was supposed to be stocking shelves, so I glanced over to see if Dad was watching. He was waiting on a customer as I slipped outside.

"What's the big deal?" I asked.

"You'll see. Over here, behind the garbage cans."

I followed him.

Leon opened a paper bag. "Fireworks for tonight. Not just sparklers and snappers, either. These are the good ones." He held up a cardboard cylinder with a stick coming out of the bottom. "Get a load of this."

"Wow, is that a rocket? The kind that explodes way up in the air?"

"Sure is. I got three of them. And a couple of cherry bombs, too. If you come over, we can set them off behind the school after it gets dark."

"Where did you get all this?"

"My cousin, Bill. I have to give him my allowance for the next three weeks to pay for them. You should see all the stuff he has. He and his friends are driving out to the lake tonight to set them off."

"This is great!" I said. "I can't believe we get to see fireworks again." I had only been six years old when the war started, but I could still remember fireworks. They were banned all during the war because of the blackouts. We couldn't even have firecrackers because the flame from a match might be seen from the air. Once, during a drill, I had opened our blackout shade just a slit to peek out. Our neighborhood air-raid warden saw it and gave me holy heck.

I was glad Leon had fireworks, but I wasn't going to stand close to him when he set them off. Leon was a good friend, but he didn't always think things through. "You sure you know how to do this?"

"It's a cinch. You just set them up and light the fuse. Bill told me how."

I could picture Leon lighting the wrong end of something and blowing us to smithereens. "Maybe we should take your stuff to the lake with your cousin."

"First off, Bill doesn't want us hanging around, because he'll have his girlfriend with him. Besides, my sister would never let me go if she knew they were doing fireworks. Our mom always used to tell us you can blow your hand off with these things." Leon lived with his father and his older sister, Phyllis, who was supposed to keep track of him.

"Yeah, my mom says the same thing," I said. "She wouldn't let me go, either. I gotta get back to work, Leon. I'll come over to your house after dinner."

I tried to keep the door from squeaking as I went back in. Then Mrs. Baumgartner came barreling in right behind me and let it slam. Dad looked up from behind the meat counter in the back, but I ducked into the canned vegetable aisle before he saw me. I had just opened a case of canned corn before Leon had called me outside. Now I moved the cans of corn on the shelf to one side and checked the new price that Mom had written on the case. I marked the new cans with a grease pencil and pushed them to the back of the shelf. It was two cents more than before, so I had to wipe off the price on the old cans and re-mark them before stacking them in front of the new stuff.

Mrs. Baumgartner came down my aisle. "Good morning, Norman. I'll take one of those cans before you raise the price. Eight cents is more than enough to pay for corn." Mrs. Baumgartner was always looking for a bargain.

"Yes, ma'am," I said, handing it to her. Dad's rule was that the customers are always right, even when they're wrong, so I didn't argue with her.

I finished up the corn and went to get a carton of canned peas from behind the meat counter. Mrs. Baumgartner was looking in the display case with a scowl on her face. "Your chicken livers are fifteen cents a pound, Walter? That's highway robbery. Morton's Grocery had them for ten cents this morning."

My father was wrapping hot dogs. "Then why didn't you buy chicken livers from Morton, Mrs. Baumgartner?"

"Because he was out of them, that's why."

Dad tied string around the package and slid it across the glass to his other customer. Then he leaned on the counter and smiled. "When I'm out of chicken livers, Mrs. Baumgartner, I sell them for a *penny* a pound."

Mrs. Baumgartner looked huffy for a second, then almost smiled. "All right, Walter, give me a half pound of your gold-plated chicken livers."

That's why everybody liked Dad. He could always joke people out of their bad moods. I would have told old Mrs. Baumgartner to go fly a kite, which is why I didn't have to wait on customers very often. I liked stocking shelves because I could be a million miles away, thinking about things I'd rather be doing, like drawing pictures of cars or playing baseball, the same as I did in school. Last year, my fifth grade teacher, Miss Dworetsky, nicknamed me "Dreamin' Norman" because I was always off in my own world. She also called me "Norman Rockwell" because anytime I wasn't daydreaming, I was doodling in my notebook.

When I grow up, I want to be either a baseball player or an artist, but I've never told my family. Dad thinks I'll work full-time in the family business after high school. He's always telling Mr. Knapp, the sign painter, that he'll need a "Schmidt and Son" sign painted one of these days. Heck, I could paint that sign myself, if I wanted to work here, which I don't.

The screen door slammed every couple of minutes now. People were coming in to get hot dogs and chopped meat to make hamburgers for their Fourth of July cookouts. Dad had the chopped meat on special for the holiday—fourteen cents a pound. I supposed Mrs. Baumgartner would want that for less, too.

4

This was the first Independence Day since the war ended, so people were celebrating in a big way. Meat rationing was over. Now people could buy as much as they wanted, so they went hog wild.

We had a line of customers that wound from the meat counter to the potato chips and pretzels up by the front door. Ray, our only employee, was ringing up sales every few minutes. Usually Mom would have been helping Dad wait on customers, but she had taken my younger sister, Ellie, to march with her Brownie troop in the Fourth of July parade. If Dad didn't need me in the store, I'd be marching, too, with my Boy Scout troop. Ellie got off easy. She hardly ever had to do store work.

"Norm," Dad called. "Give me a hand back here."

I thought I'd get stuck waiting on customers. That's not why he wanted me, though. "I'm running low on chopped meat. I need you to make me some."

"Sure, Dad." What a relief. I didn't get to use the meat grinder very often. If I worked for somebody else, I probably wouldn't get to use it at all. But in a family business, everybody did what was needed, no questions asked. Dad had taught me how to use the meat grinder when I was nine.

Dad brought out a heavy tray of beef chunks and set it on the thick wooden table that had the grinder bolted to it.

"Call me as soon as you're done with this, Norm. I need it—*mach schnell.* We're selling more chopped meat than I expected."

I started the motor, filled the tray on top with beef,

and pushed the pieces over so they fell though the hole in the tray down into the hopper. From there, a steel corkscrew grabbed the meat and moved it through a long tube. At the end, it was sliced by a rotating blade and pushed through a plate that had small holes.

Ever since I was a little kid, playing in the back room while my parents worked, I had liked to watch the meat come out of the grinder. The long, thin ropes of beef looped back and forth over themselves like the yarn wig on Ellie's Raggedy Ann doll.

I shoved the meat down into the hopper with a wooden plunger, then refilled the tray. I didn't mind missing the parade. It looked like rain. I hoped it wouldn't rain tonight, though. The fireworks might be hard to light if they got wet. Maybe they'd just fizzle. Boy, that sure would be disappointing.

The grinder motor slowed down, so I poked with the plunger, but it didn't help. I could see a piece of gristle that had gotten caught in the corkscrew. I grabbed the end of it and tugged. I must have loosened whatever was caught, because the hunk of gristle suddenly tugged back—hard.

I'm not sure when I realized that I couldn't pull my hand out. Whenever it was, it was too late. I don't know why I didn't flip the switch. I guess my brain couldn't believe what was happening. Dad had asked me to give him a hand, and that's exactly what I was doing. I was fast becoming part of the fourteen-cent chopped meat special—which, I'm told, was not a big seller for the rest of the day.

Chapter **2**

I must have screamed bloody murder. Dad came running in and turned off the grinder. He looked into the hopper, but didn't even try to pull my hand out.

He yelled to Ray. "Call Dr. Cupernail. Norm's been hurt bad."

Some of the customers rushed in to help. A woman asked me if she could get me something. I said the first thing that came into my mind, "A cherry soda from Sager's, please." She ran two doors down to Sager's soda fountain and brought the drink back in a glass with ice. It tasted cold and sweet. I didn't feel any pain, but I must have looked pretty bad, because Ray stepped behind my stool and stood with his arms wrapped tight around my middle to hold me steady.

Dr. Cupernail arrived fast. At least I think it was fast. Time was doing funny things in my head. He was our family doctor and lived nearby, so he knew the way. "Well, Norman, what have you gotten yourself into here?"

"A meat grinder," I said.

"I can see that." Dr. Cupernail put his medical bag on the table and took off his suit jacket. He was a big man, and sweating from the rush of getting here. He got serious when he looked down into the hopper. "You tell me if anything hurts, Norman." He pressed gently on my arm, starting at the elbow.

"Feel any pain?"

"No."

He pressed lower on my arm and looked at me. "Now?"

I shook my head.

He rolled up his sleeve and moved farther down. "How about now?"

"It doesn't hurt."

"I'm just going to see if I can wiggle your hand around a bit and get you out of this. You be sure to tell me if I hurt you."

He worked at it for a few seconds, then gave up.

"I didn't feel it," I said.

Dr. Cupernail patted my shoulder. "That's all right, Norman."

"We can take the whole grinder apart," Dad said. "Maybe he's caught his finger in the corkscrew."

Dr. Cupernail adjusted his glasses and looked closely at the end where the meat comes out. "Walter, I'm not going to try to get Norman out of this. The way he's clamped in there is keeping the bleeding under control. We'll let them extricate him in surgery. The boy's going into shock, so we need to get him to the hospital right away. Can we detach the grinder in one piece from the motor?"

"Sure. It all comes apart." Dad's voice was funny— low, like he was trying not to cry. Dad never cried.

"You think they'll let me out of the hospital by dinner?" I asked. "I have plans for tonight."

Dr. Cupernail checked my heart with his stethoscope. "Let's take things one at a time, Norm. Just one thing at a time."

I was kind of in and out after that. Some guy told me, "Don't worry, kid. Everything's gonna be okay."

I knew it wasn't going to be okay. Don't ask me how, but I knew. I leaned back against Ray and closed my eyes. I heard the familiar sounds of the grinder being taken off the motor. We did it at least twice every day to clean it. That was another one of my jobs. The thing weighed about forty pounds, so Dad always had to lug it over to the sink for me.

When they finally got the grinder loose, Dad and Dr. Cupernail carried it between them, while I walked close behind it. Ray couldn't go with us. He had to stay and run the store. As we passed him I reached out to stop Dad and the doctor. "Wait! I gotta tell Ray something."

"What is it, Norm?" Ray asked, leaning close.

"Whatever you do, don't sell that chopped meat I made," I whispered. "You gotta do a new batch."

Ray had tears in his eyes. "Yeah, Norm. Okay. Don't worry."

They say Mrs. Baumgartner fainted after we went by, taking the whole grapefruit pyramid down with her. Boy, I sure wish I'd turned around to see that.

I remember sitting in the back seat of a car

between Dad and the doctor. The grinder was on my lap, weighing me down, but my hand still didn't hurt. "Dad?"

"What, Norman?"

"Ray can't make more chopped meat because we took the grinder."

"It doesn't matter, Norm. Just rest."

"Okay." I sank back into a fuzzy mist. Dr. Cupernail was listening to my heart again.

Then I suddenly remembered about the fireworks and how Mom always said I'd blow my hand off. Here I'd gone and lost my hand in the stupid meat grinder. I didn't have to wait for them to give me the bad news at the hospital. I knew I wasn't going to have a left hand when this was over. I started to laugh.

Dad put his hand on my shoulder. "Norm, what's the matter?"

"It wasn't the fireworks, like Mom thought."

"What?"

"The hand. I never got near Leon's fireworks, but it's gone anyway."

"He's not making any sense," Dad said.

Dr. Cupernail nodded as he folded up his stethoscope. "Shock," he whispered.

But I was making sense in my own head. It's like the old saying that you'll die when it's your time to go. Well, me and my left hand had two different times to go. If I hadn't lost that hand in the meat grinder, it would have gotten blown off by Leon's fireworks for sure. No matter how far away from him I stood, one of those darn rockets would have aimed itself right at me.

Even in my foggy state, it all became perfectly clear. When I came into this world, my left hand had a return-trip ticket for July 4, 1946. I was just glad the rest of me wasn't going back to heaven with the hand.

I would have explained my theory to Dad and Dr. Cupernail, but that's when I passed out.

Chapter **3**

When I woke up, people were calling my name. Their voices were all broken up like echoes. I could make out shapes of light, but I couldn't tell what anything was. Then one voice came out of the rest. "Wake up, honey. It's over."

After I blinked a few times I could see Mom sitting beside my bed. "You look fuzzy," I said.

She smiled and squeezed my hand. "I think you're the fuzzy one, Normie. You've been through a lot."

"I have?"

There was a tall man in a white coat standing behind Mom. He leaned toward me. "I'm Dr. Zeigler, Norman. You did just fine."

"I did? What did I do?" Then I remembered. I turned to Mom. "The meat grinder. I'm sorry I broke it, Mom. Is Dad mad at me?"

"It's all right," Mom said. "You didn't break it and your father isn't mad."

"Oh, that's good." Then I remembered my hand. My whole left arm was under the covers. I couldn't tell if I still had my hand or not. I started to reach over to feel for it, then stopped. I wasn't sure if I wanted to know. I didn't want to look at it. Not yet.

"You came through the surgery very nicely, Norman."

"Thank you." What was he talking about? I didn't do anything. I was asleep, for Pete's sake.

"You're probably feeling a little woozy now, but you'll be getting stronger each day." The doctor turned to Mom. "I'll leave you two alone, Mrs. Schmidt, but don't stay too long. We should let him rest. It's been a long day for everybody."

"All right, Doctor," Mom said.

"Who was he?" I asked, after the doctor was gone. "What happened to Dr. Cupernail?"

"Dr. Zeigler is the surgeon. He's the one who got you out of the meat grinder. Dr. Cupernail doesn't do that sort of thing."

I wondered how many doctors *did* do meat grinders. It wasn't something you'd put on the sign outside your office. I wanted to ask Mom about my hand, but I asked her about the parade instead.

"We did not see too much of it," she said. "Mrs. Friehofer came to find me and tell me about your accident, so I left Ellie with Mrs. Muller, her Brownie leader, and came right here."

"Does everybody know?"

"I imagine word is getting around. News spreads like wildfire in a small town like Lake Carmel. Pastor Reinhold heard about you and came here. He waited with your father and me while you were in the operating room."

"Is Dad here?" I asked.

"He's downstairs waiting for me."

"Can he come up?"

"It's late, Norm." Mom leaned over and kissed my forehead. "And you're looking sleepy. I think I should go. Are you going to be all right by yourself?"

"I guess so."

She handed me a cord with a knob at the end. "You push this button if you need the nurse."

"Okay."

Mom was almost through the door when I called out to her. "Mom?"

She turned. "Yes, Norm? You want me to stay with you?"

"No, I just want to know what time it is."

She looked at her watch. "Eight-thirty."

"What day? Is it still the Fourth of July?"

"Yes, it is."

"What happened in the Giants' doubleheader today? Did they beat the Dodgers?"

"I don't know, Norm. I didn't hear anything about it."

Boy, that was something. Mom and I were both huge Giants fans. It would take something pretty big to keep Mom from getting the score of a game, especially one with their biggest rival, the Dodgers.

"You're sure you'll be all right by yourself tonight?" she asked.

"I'm fine, Mom. I'll see you tomorrow."

I could hear her footsteps going down the hall. If she had waited one more minute, I would have asked her to stay with me, but I didn't want to be a sissy. I wished I could go home with her, though. I could picture Leon sneaking his fireworks out of the house to set them off without me. I heard a few booms and thought about going to the window to try and see some fireworks, but I was too tired to get out of bed. Thinking made me sleepy. I closed my eyes and conked out for the night.

The next morning some lady came in and sat next to my bed. "You're Norman Schmidt?"

"Yes, ma'am." She had a clipboard and looked like she was going to ask me questions. Instead, she introduced herself as Miss Albright, the social worker, and asked me if I had any questions.

"About what?"

She cleared her throat, unclipped her papers, and lined them up before clamping them down again. "Well, I thought you might wonder what it's going to be like to manage with one hand."

Well, that pretty much took care of my biggest question. I felt as if she had kicked me in the stomach. Okay, the hand was gone. I knew it all along. I was just kidding myself, thinking Dr. Zeigler could have saved it. There was a roaring sound in my ears. I saw Miss Albright's lips moving. Then the roaring died down and I heard her say, "Norman? Are you all right? Do you want to ask me anything?"

I just looked at her. I couldn't think of a question.

Miss Albright waited a minute or two for me to say something, then forged ahead. "Next summer you'll go into New York City to be fitted with a prosthesis."

That got my attention. "A hook? You mean I'll have to wear a hook?"

"You'll *want* to wear one, Norman. Then you'll be able to do lots more things, like tie your shoelaces, button up your shirt, and cut your meat. The new prostheses are quite amazing. You can even light a cigarette with them."

"I don't smoke," I said. Once, I had sneaked a cigarette out behind the store. I got so sick, I thought I was going to die. I wouldn't be lighting any more cigarettes—hook or no hook.

"I thought of a question," I said.

"Good. You can ask me anything, Norman. Anything at all."

"Can you catch a baseball with a hook?"

Miss Albright blinked. "Well, no. I don't think so."

"What about batting? Do they have special hooks for that?"

Miss Albright leaned forward in her seat and smiled. "The hook is meant for practical purposes, Norman. We call them A.D.L.—activities of daily living."

"Baseball is an activity of *my* daily living. I'm going to be a pitcher when I grow up."

She adjusted her papers in the clipboard again. "I'm sure there are many sports you can enjoy even before you get your hook. Croquet, for instance. You wouldn't have to catch a ball—just hit it around with the mallet. And then there's tennis. Oh . . . but that wouldn't work because you have to have two hands to serve the ball. But there must be lots of other sports. Ping-Pong! But, no, we have that same problem of serving the ball, don't we?"

I yawned, pretending to be sleepy. I couldn't take

much more of Miss Albright. According to her, from now until I got my hook, I'd be tripping over my shoelaces, running around with my shirt flapping open, ripping my meat with my teeth, and playing *croquet,* for Pete's sake. I closed my eyes.

"Um, Norman? Are you falling asleep?" she asked.

I snored softly.

"We weren't quite finished, but . . ." I heard her chair scrape against the floor, then the click of high heels going down the hall. I squinted out of one eye to make sure she was really gone. She was.

Okay, *now* I was worried. What stuff couldn't I do anymore? My mind started racing through a regular day. Eating breakfast would be okay, because I usually had cereal. If it was eggs and bacon, I could pick up the bacon and eat it with my fingers. Putting jam on the toast would be a mess, though. Then afterward, brushing my teeth. How would I get the toothpaste on the brush? Maybe I'd just skip brushing my teeth. I did that half the time anyway.

I wondered how much of my arm was still there. I reached under the covers and touched it up by the elbow. Then I slid my fingers down until I felt the edge of a bandage about halfway to my wrist. I stopped because I caught a glimpse of somebody in the doorway. I closed my eyes, in case it was Miss Albright.

"Pssst! Hey, Norm!"

"Leon? How did you get in here? They don't allow any kids."

He shrugged. "I just walked through the front door and kept walking. Nobody said anything."

"Well, you better duck if anyone comes in. Who brought you over here?"

"Nobody. I rode my bike." Ever since Leon's mother died, his father paid more attention to his whiskey than to his kids. Phyllis was so busy with her friends, she didn't know where Leon was half the time. He probably could be gone a couple of days before anybody got worked up about it. Leon walked around to the other side of the bed. "So it's the left one, huh?"

"Yeah," I said. That was pretty obvious, since my right hand was out in the open.

"Does it hurt?"

"It's kind of tingly, like when you hit your funny bone. It almost feels like my hand is still there—only asleep."

Leon made a face. "You mean your whole hand is gone? That's creepy. What does it look like?"

"I don't know."

"You haven't looked? That would've been the first thing I did after I came out of the ether. What's the matter? Are you chicken?"

"Hey! You take *your* hand off with a meat grinder and see how soon *you* want to look at it."

Leon raised his hands. "Okay, *okay*! I take it back—calling you chicken, I mean. But I still would have looked first thing." He wandered around the room, pulling out the drawers on the nightstand and fiddling with the cord on the window shade. Then he spotted the bedpan and did a little dance across the room, singing the "Chiquita Banana" song, holding the pan on top of his head.

"Cut it out. Somebody's going to hear you." I couldn't help smiling, though. It cheered me up to see Leon.

He put down the bedpan and came over to me. "Listen, Norm, if it feels like your hand is still there, maybe part of it is."

"No, they told me it's gone. I'm not even sure how much of my arm is left."

"Want me to check it for you? Tell you what it looks like?"

"No! Well . . . maybe . . . okay. But don't touch it!"

He pulled back the blanket. "It's bandaged."

"I *know* that. How much is there?"

"How much bandage?"

"No, how much arm."

"It's hard to tell. Hold both arms out so I can compare them."

Without thinking, I did what he said. And there it was, right out in plain sight, all covered in adhesive tape with gauze padding sticking out on the edge. It was shorter than my other arm, and the end where the hand should be was rounded off, like the end of a baseball bat.

"Looks like you still have all of your arm," Leon said. "They must have cut it off right about here." He drew an imaginary line with his finger across my right wrist, just above the little bone that bumps out on the side.

I didn't say anything. I felt like I was going to throw up. I put my arms down but kept the left one on top of the covers this time, so I could get used to seeing it. I took some deep breaths until I felt better. "So, did you set off the fireworks last night?" I asked when I could talk again.

"Nah. Phyllis looked under my bed and found them. She took everything—said I'd blow my hand off." Leon ducked his head. Then he looked up and grinned. "Too bad I didn't, huh? If I lost my right hand, we could have shared mittens."

We both laughed a little at that. Then I thought about something.

"Hey, Leon, do you remember that sailor who lost his hand in the war? He used to come into the store."

"Yeah, he wore a hook. Are you gonna get one of those things?"

"Yes, but not until next summer. Anyway, I used to hide behind the shelves and stare at him."

"So?"

"Well, I was wondering. Do you think this is payback because I did that?"

"You stare at some guy with a hook and then God lops your hand off?"

"Yeah. Kind of makes sense, doesn't it?"

Leon thought about it for a minute, then shook his head. "Nah. You didn't do anything to the guy. You were just looking. Everybody stares at a cripple. You can't help it."

"Thanks a bunch," I said.

"I wasn't talking about you, Norm, but it's the truth. People are going to stare. You'll just have to get used to it."

"You know the first thing I'm going to do when I get my hook, Leon?"

"No, what?"

"I'm going to conk you over the head with it."

That was one A.D.L. that Miss Albright probably hadn't thought about.

Chapter 4

I was in the hospital for a whole week. Mom came to visit me every night around seven, but Dad was always too busy. I had a lot of time to just lie around feeling sorry for myself, especially at dinnertime when a nurse dropped off my tray and left. There was usually some tough meat that I couldn't cut up myself, but I could pick that up in my hand.

The second night I got a Dixie Cup for dessert, which perked up my spirits because I love ice cream. I tried to steady the cup with the end of my left arm while I pulled on the tab, but it sent shock waves through me. When I tried holding the cup down with my elbow, it flipped off my tray and rolled out into the hall. I saw the thing sitting out there against the wall while dozens of pairs of feet walked by it. Pretty soon the melted ice cream oozed out into a puddle on the floor. That's when it hit me. From now on, the simplest things would be impossible. I couldn't help it. I stared at that blob of ice cream and cried.

—◆—

The night before I was going home, Dr. Zeigler came in to change the bandage for the last time. "Your stump is healing nicely, Norman."

"That's good," I said. My stump. So that's what you called it. I didn't like the word. I was going to call it my arm. I never watched him change the bandage, because I didn't want to see what was under it.

"Tomorrow's the big day, Norm. You must be glad to be going home."

"I guess so."

"I'll need to see you every week for the first month, then every couple of weeks after that to see how you're coming along. Do you have any questions?"

"I guess not."

Dr. Zeigler sat on the edge of my bed. "You're doing a lot of guessing, here. Are you worried about how things will work out?"

"I guess . . . I mean, yeah, sure, I'm worried about some things."

"Like what, for instance?"

"Well, when Miss Albright was telling me I'd have to get a hook, I asked if I'd be able to catch a baseball with it, and she said no. I want to be a pitcher when I grow up, but I guess . . . I mean, now I can't."

"Wait a minute," Dr. Zeigler said. "You've never heard of Pete Gray?"

"Who?"

"Pete Gray, the one-handed outfielder for the St. Louis Browns."

"He only has one hand and he plays in the majors?"

"He did last year. They brought him up from a minor-league team when so many of the players went off to war. Now that the servicemen are home, he got sent back down to the minors, but he did a good job while he was there."

"So could he catch with his hook?"

"He didn't wear a hook, at least not for baseball. I saw him play in a doubleheader at Yankee Stadium last year. He hit well—scored twice and drove in a couple of runs. He was a good outfielder, too. Not much got past him."

"But how did he catch? You have to squeeze your hand to keep the ball in the glove. Could a hook do that? I was thinking I could glue my glove onto the hook, because that's the main thing I need it for. Miss Albright said I could use the hook for lighting cigarettes, but I don't smoke."

Dr. Zeigler laughed. "Whoa, slow down, Norman. You'll have to excuse Miss Albright. We're all used to working with veterans since the war, so we think in terms of what a grown man might want to do instead of a boy. I don't think the prosthesis was designed to catch a ball, though. It will be quite a while before you get yours, so if I were you, I'd start learning how to play baseball without it."

"You think I could?"

"I told you, Pete Gray didn't wear a prosthesis when he played. I can't remember exactly how he did it, but I imagine he worked until he found a way to throw and catch with one hand, the same as you're trying to think it out in your head right now. You keep on doing that and you'll be just fine. Start practicing when you get home. See what works best for you."

"Yes, sir, I will."

Dr. Zeigler patted my back and got up. "And another thing, Norman. I've worked with a lot of men who lost hands in the war. Some of them have done very well, and others haven't made much progress. You know what makes the difference?"

I shook my head.

"The ones who succeed don't give themselves the option of failing. Whatever they attempt, they tell themselves they're going to be able to do it. And they keep trying until they figure it out. Does that make sense to you?"

"I guess . . ." Dr. Zeigler's raised eyebrow stopped me. "Yes, sir. It makes a lot of sense."

He paused at the door and looked back. "You may not believe this right now, Norman, but this isn't the end of the world. In some ways you've got it all over your friends. They're just happy-go-lucky, going through one day after another without thinking. You've been given a chance to really look inside yourself and discover what makes you tick."

"Yes, sir," I said, but I thought he was nuts. I could have looked inside myself without losing a hand. But he understood how I felt about baseball. And if there was a one-handed guy who had played in the majors, maybe there was hope for me.

That night I had a hard time falling asleep because I was trying to figure out how Pete Gray kept getting the glove on and off his good hand. I wanted to be a pitcher instead of an outfielder, but I'd still need a glove to catch, and I'd have to get rid of it to throw. When I finally dozed off, I dreamed I pitched a perfect game for the New York Giants. The whole town of Lake Carmel drove to the Polo Grounds in New York in a caravan of buses to see me play. Afterward they carried me around the field on their shoulders. All except for old Mrs. Baumgartner, who was too cheap to pay for the bus ride.

Mom was the one who picked me up the next morning. I had to wait while she had a long talk with Dr. Zeigler without me. She was pretty quiet on the way home.

"You want to go into the store to see your father?" Mom asked, as we pulled into the store parking lot.

"Not really." I was mad that Dad hadn't visited me in the hospital. You'd think in a whole week he could have made it to Mt. Kisco once. He couldn't have been busy every single night. We took the door on the right and climbed the stairs to our apartment. Ellie was in the living room playing with her Princess Elizabeth doll.

"Hi, Normie." She had a funny smile on her face. She came over and kissed me on the cheek.

"Hey!" I said. "What was *that* for?"

"I'm just glad you're home."

Mom put her purse on the dining-room table and grabbed her apron. "The parking lot was crowded with customers. I need to get downstairs and help your father. Ellie can get me if you need me for something. All right?"

"Sure, Mom."

"I'll bring up some cold cuts for lunch. You want anything special, Norm?"

"Roast beef," I said. "And dark pumpernickel bread."

Mom blew me a kiss before she ran down the stairs to the store.

When I looked up, Ellie was staring at me. Leon had been right. It was starting already. "What do you think you're looking at?"

"Nothing. Sorry." She turned away, brushing at her Princess Elizabeth doll's hair so hard, I thought she'd make the thing bald.

"Get me a bottle of soda," I ordered.

"Okay." She bounced up off the couch and ran into the kitchen. A couple of minutes later she came back in and handed me a cold Coca-Cola, the glass bottle already sweating from the hot air.

"Now get me a chocolate chip cookie."

She disappeared into the kitchen again and came back with a cookie.

I let her just get settled in again before I said, "I want some potato chips."

"All right." She put down her doll and headed for the kitchen.

"Ellie, come back here."

She stopped and turned. "What?"

"What the heck is wrong with you?"

"Nothing. Why?"

"I'm trying to get your goat, and you're being *nice* to me."

She gave me that weird smile again. It looked like something a little kid would draw with a crayon—too wide at the corners, with every single tooth showing. "You're my brother. Why wouldn't I be nice?"

"You've never, ever been nice to me, that's why.

When you were a baby, the first thing you did when Mom brought you home was throw up on me."

"You couldn't remember that. You were only three years old."

"I was old enough to know you were going to make my life miserable. So what's going on? Why are you acting like Shirley Temple?"

"Mommy said I couldn't pick fights with you anymore." Ellie plopped on the couch so hard, Princess Elizabeth did a double somersault onto the rug. "It's driving me nuts! You've always been such a spoiled brat, Norman Schmidt. And now you're going to be even worse because of your . . . you know—" She waggled her left hand at me. "Anyway, from now on I'm only going to be nice to you when Mommy and Daddy are around."

"That's a relief," I said. "You were giving me the creeps. I thought my real sister had been kidnapped by Gypsies."

"You wish," Ellie said, sticking her tongue out at me.

I picked up the latest copy of *Life* magazine and sat at the table flipping through the pictures. I was looking for a baseball story, maybe something about the Giants and Dodgers game I missed, but the only thing about baseball I could find was a laxative ad with a picture of a kid about my age in the batter's box. The caption said, "You'd never think that peppy little slugger was sluggish yesterday." No wonder they had to use some poor kid in the ad. No real baseball player would advertise the fact that he was constipated, for Pete's sake.

Ellie had retrieved Princess Elizabeth and gone back to playing, but pretty soon I could tell she was watching me again. "Cut it out!"

"What? I'm not doing anything."

"You're staring. Come over here and take a good look, so you can get it out of your system."

Ellie slipped into the seat next to me and looked at my bandaged arm. "Does it hurt?"

"Not so much." I didn't tell her about the weird tingly feeling. That was none of her business.

"Was your operation awful?"

"How should I know? I was out cold."

"I thought Mom might bring you home from the hospital in a wheelchair."

"Why would I need a wheelchair? It's my hand, not my foot."

"I know. I just thought you might be weak or something."

"Well, I'm not weak. I'm normal, okay? Just call me Normal Norman. I could beat you up with one hand tied behind my back."

Ellie giggled, then got serious again. "Daddy's been really upset about this, you know."

"Oh, yeah. He was so upset, he couldn't bother to come see me."

"No, I mean it, Norman. That first night when they came home from the hospital? Daddy stayed outside while Mommy came upstairs. Mrs. Muller was waiting here with me. When she left, I watched Daddy talking with her down in the parking lot for a couple of minutes. Then she drove off, and you know what?" Ellie's eyes were wide and shiny with tears.

"What?"

She dropped her voice to a whisper even though nobody was around. "Daddy went out behind the store and cried. Have you ever seen him cry?"

"Uh-uh."

"Me neither. Not even at Oma's funeral. That's what made me so scared. He's been different ever since your accident."

"Different how?"

"Kind of sad and quiet. I haven't heard him crack a single joke all week."

"This is a *bad* thing? Dad not telling his corny jokes?"

Ellie wrapped her arms tight around herself. "It's awful, Normie. Daddy just isn't the same anymore."

Well, that makes two of us, I thought.

Chapter 5

*R*ight before dinner, I saw Dad for the first time since the accident. I was sitting at the table while Ellie helped Mom bring in the food from the kitchen. Dad was standing in the doorway to the dining room. "How are you feeling, Norm?"

"Okay."

"That's good." He just stood there, looking everywhere but at my arm. I didn't know what to say, and Dad didn't seem to know, either. Then Leon came bounding up the stairs and broke the silence. Dad took his seat at the table.

Nobody was surprised to see Leon. He usually showed up just in time for a meal because Mom was a good cook. Phyllis's big claim to fame was a Spam and lima bean casserole she learned to make in Home Ec. Even their dog wouldn't eat it.

Our dog, Knocky, lived in pooch heaven. A butcher's dog ate better than most people. There were always bones and meat scraps for him. He was under the table now, waiting for anything that came his way. I could tell because I heard the knocking sound his leg made against the floor when he scratched himself.

Leon speared a slice of roast pork from the platter Mom was passing around, then reached for a second, but looked at Mom before taking it. She nodded. "Go ahead, Leon. There's plenty for everybody. The war's over, you know."

I loved Mom's roasts. She always cooked them in the oven in the back room of the store, so they filled the whole building with their delicious smell. Dad sold twice as many roasts on a day when Mom was cooking one.

I rocked the side of my fork on my slice of meat, trying to cut through it. But I was barely making a dent.

Dad reached for my plate. "Give it here, Norman. I'll cut that up for you."

"He needs to learn how to do that himself," Mom said.

"Now how's he supposed to do that, Lucille? You need two hands to cut meat." Dad took my plate, then handed it back with the meat cut in tiny cubes.

"It doesn't have to be *that* small," I said. "I still have teeth." Ellie kicked my leg under the table and glared at me.

Dad didn't say anything, but his face was red and he was shoving his food down fast. I realized that he had cut my meat in baby pieces, the way he did it when we were little. Leon got it, too. He looked at my plate and grinned, then kicked my other leg. I was going to start wearing shin guards to meals.

Dad pushed away from the table. "I need to fill out orders in the store."

"I made cherry kuchen," Mom said.

"No time now. Maybe later."

I had never heard Dad turn down anything with cherries before. He always said the cherry season was so short, you hardly got to taste them before they were gone.

Nobody said much after Dad left. This wasn't like our usual meals with everybody talking at once. Even Leon kept his mouth shut for a change. After dessert, Mom asked Ellie to clear the table. Leon and I got up and headed for the living room.

"Norman, you need to empty the garbage," Mom said.

"How can I do that with one hand?"

She handed me the kitchen garbage pail. "Same way as always. You walk down the stairs, go out back, open the can, and put the bag of garbage into it."

This was one job I was sure I'd never have to do again. I hated the way the juicy stuff seeped through the paper bag, and the maggots made me gag. "How will I get the top off the garbage can? It fits too tight."

"C'mon, Norm," Leon said. "I'll help you."

"Stay where you are," Mom said. "Norman can figure this out for himself."

"But I'm tired," I complained.

"Then you'll go right to bed after you empty the garbage."

I glared at her. She glared back. I could tell she wasn't going to give in, so I took the pail in my right arm and started down the stairs. "I don't think Dr.

Zeigler would want me doing this," I called over my shoulder.

No answer.

"I just got out of the hospital, you know."

Still no answer. By now, I was at the bottom of the stairs. I went around to the back, set down the pail, and yanked hard at the top of the garbage can. It came off so easily, I almost fell over. So much for *that* excuse. I stuffed the new bag on top of the old, slimy, maggoty ones and slammed the top on before the stink reached my nose.

When I got back to the kitchen, all Mom said was "Thank you, Norman." That was one good thing about Mom. She wasn't a gloater. She was tough, though. I wondered what a person would have to do around here to get out of emptying the garbage.

The next morning, I got dressed, but when I saw myself in the bathroom mirror, I didn't want my arm hanging out in plain sight. I dug around in my closet and found a long-sleeved flannel shirt. It was kind of hot, but the sleeve covered up the whole bandage. It took forever to button the thing. I had to hold the shirt against my chest with my left arm while I fished the buttons through the buttonholes. Then I ended up with an extra button at the bottom. I put on my shoes, but I couldn't tie the laces. By now I was starving, so I headed for the kitchen. Dad was already down in the store, but Ellie was there.

"It's really hot outside," she said. "Why are you dressed for winter?"

"What are you, a fashion expert all of a sudden?"

Mom came in from the living room. "Your sister's right, Norm. You'll swelter in that shirt."

"I'm fine. I can't do my shoelaces, though."

I sat down and Mom got on her knees to tie the laces. "You have to learn how to do this yourself, Norman."

"I know. Maybe when I get the hook. You can't do it with one hand."

Mom gave a final yank to my right lace. "You won't get the hook for a year. You want your mother tagging along to tie your laces when they come undone?"

"Well, what am I supposed to do?"

"Think of tying shoes as a puzzle. You're good at figuring things out." As she got up, she tugged on my collar. "And I don't want to see this shirt again until there's snow in the air." Mom grabbed her apron and went down to the store.

Ellie was making her own breakfast. I was heading for the refrigerator, but she beat me to it, opening the door right in my face. Without thinking, I put out my left arm to stop it. The door hit hard on the end of my arm, where the stitches were. It was more like an electric shock than ordinary pain. It took my breath away, as if somebody had punched me in the gut.

"What's the matter, Normie? You look like you're going to throw up."

"Nothing's wrong," I gasped. I went back to my room so she wouldn't see the tears. I felt dizzy, so I sat on my bed until the pain let up. By now I was sweating bullets. I took off the flannel shirt, pulled on a short-sleeved T-shirt, then waited until I heard Ellie go downstairs before I left my room.

I fixed myself a bowl of Wheaties—Breakfast of Champions. Yeah, that was me, all right. Knocky came over and sat on my left side because I usually petted him with that hand while I ate with my right. He kept bumping me with his nose, so I finally patted him with my arm, being careful not to hit the end of it. Knocky didn't seem to notice there was no hand. His tail drummed the floor. When I stopped, he bumped me again, asking for more.

I ate the last of my cereal and went out to the garage, where I kept all of my sports stuff. I left Knocky upstairs, whining. I wanted to figure out how much I was going to be able to do with one hand, and I didn't want anybody watching—not even my dog.

The first things I saw hanging on the wall were my slingshot and my bow and arrow. I'd made the sling-shot myself from a forked branch that I carved into the perfect shape with notches at the tips for the sling, which I cut from an old inner tube. I was really good with it. I could knock a tin can off a fence from fifty feet away.

I put the slingshot in the crook of my left elbow and tested it out with a few trial pulls. If I squeezed tight, it seemed to hold. Then I set up a can on the fence in the far back end of the yard, found a stone, and took aim. It looked strange, because I usually had the full length of my arm to sight down. This was only about a foot from my face. I pulled back slowly, holding the slingshot steady as I centered the can between the two forks. Suddenly the slingshot came loose and smashed into my cheek, just under my left eye. From the way it hurt, I could tell I'd probably get a shiner. I had one more thing to add to the list of stuff I couldn't do anymore. I didn't even bother with the bow and arrow.

I tried my football next. I could throw it up in the air with one hand, but catching it wasn't so easy. It kept bouncing off my hand. Then I tried trapping it against my body. That worked once in a while, but in a game, you wouldn't have a ball coming straight down from above very often. I might be able to use my left arm to help, but I didn't want to take a chance of hurting it again. Still, I could see how I might be able to play football if I worked at it.

Riding my bike was a piece of cake. Heck, I rode around no-hands half the time anyway. I did a few figure eights in the parking lot, then took off down the road, turning right away onto a side street where there wouldn't be many people. It felt good to be able to do something normal again, but I couldn't figure out the best way to hold my left arm. I didn't want it dangling out in the open. I could probably put it in my pants pocket, or just hold it close to my chest so it looked like I was carrying something. I noticed some little kids playing in a yard up ahead. I didn't want to ride past them and have them staring at me, so I doubled back and headed for home.

I had planned to ask for a new bike for Christmas. I had seen a magazine ad for the new Raleigh three speed, real slick looking. The only problem was that you didn't put on the brakes by backpedaling. The new brakes were levers on the handlebars, and I could only use the one on the right side. But that could be enough to stop the bike. It would have to work, because I didn't want to be stuck riding my old clunker forever.

I had saved what I wanted to do the most for last. I parked the bike in the garage and took out my bat, ball, and glove. Right away I realized I couldn't use the left-handed glove. Okay, I'd have to ask for a new, right-handed one. I'd be sorry to give up the old glove, because I had worked a long time to get it perfectly broken in. I took a big whiff of the oiled leather before I put it back on the shelf.

At least I could practice throwing and catching. I wasn't used to catching a baseball without a glove, so I decided to start with a tennis ball. I threw it against the concrete back wall of the store and caught it on the first bounce. I tried a few more—some high, some grounders. I missed some in the beginning, but pretty soon I got the hang of it. I moved around, being a first baseman, then second, then third.

Knocky's doghouse sat sideways against the wall. One ball hit the doghouse roof by mistake and shot up at the perfect angle for a fly, so I kept doing it on purpose. It was a good thing Knocky was upstairs, or he'd be going nuts. I was backing up for a fly ball in left field when I tripped on my shoelace and fell over. Mom was right. I had to find a way to tie them myself. For now, I tucked the ends back inside the shoe.

I wasn't old enough to try out for the summer

baseball league this spring, but I was going to do it next year for sure. I loved the game even though there were a lot of other kids who played better than me. Now with just the one hand I'd have to work harder than ever. Good thing that I had almost a whole year to practice.

I wanted to try pitching, so I got a piece of chalk from Dad's workbench and drew a rectangle the size of the strike zone on the back wall of the store. Then I paced off the distance from home base to the pitcher's mound. My first few pitches were all over the place, but after a while I got the ball to settle into the sweet spot. Once I got the rhythm of it, I could do it over and over. I began keeping score, marking off the innings on the wall. I figured a few men got on base, so I kept track of that in my head.

Then I started being the radio announcer. "Norman Schmidt, the one-handed pitcher for the Giants, is firing another spectacular game. It's the bottom of the seventh, three men on base. Schmidt is checking the runners. He gives the evil eye to the man on third. Nobody steals bases when Schmidt is on the mound. Now he winds up, lets go, and . . ."

"Who are you talking to?" Leon's voice brought me out of my daydream.

"Nobody."

"What are you doing?"

"What does it look like? I'm practicing."

"For what?"

"I'm going to try out for the summer baseball team next year."

"For your information, this is a tennis ball." Leon picked up the ball and tossed it to me. "Besides, summer baseball doesn't start until next June."

"Yeah, so I'll be great by then."

"Don't be stupid. You didn't play baseball that well with two hands. How do you think you're going to make it with one?"

"If you're just going to tell me what I can't do, you can leave."

"C'mon, Norm. Everything's different now. Don't get your heart set on making the baseball team."

But it was too late. I already had. And I'd show Leon I could do it.

Chapter 6

Mom woke me up the next morning. "The new order is in downstairs, Norman. I need you to get it out on the shelves."

"I don't think I can, Mom. The cases are heavy. You need to have—"

Mom stopped me. "I know. Two hands, right? Well, Ray or your father or I can lug the cases out for you. That's six extra hands. Think that's enough?"

"I guess," I mumbled, putting the pillow over my head.

"And as soon as you're healed enough to use your left arm, I'm sure you'll be able to lift the cases yourself, Norm. The more you do, the faster you'll get back to normal."

When I'd had that week in the hospital with nothing to do but lie there and think, I had come up with one good thing about my accident. I was absolutely sure I'd get out of working in the store for the rest of the summer. That's the way things had been a few years ago. When the ending bell rang on the last day of school, I'd run out of that door with the whole summer stretching out in front of me and nothing to do but swim, play ball, and hang out. Boy, I missed that. There weren't many kids my age who had real jobs in the summer. The Schneider girls next door had to work in their father's restaurant, the Happy Valley, cleaning before opening each day, and bussing tables when the customers were there. Ronnie and Charlie Cressman worked on their father's farm, which was probably heavier work than I did, but at least they were outside most of the time. Other than that, I couldn't think of a single kid who had to do anything more than the usual chores at home.

"Norman?" Mom called from the kitchen. "Are you up?"

"Yeah," I lied. I hadn't counted on Mom's new drill-sergeant attitude. She'd given me a break the first couple of days, but now it was business as usual. So much for spending all summer on baseball. I hauled myself out of bed.

Ray gave me a big grin when I got downstairs. "Hey, Norm! Good to see you back in the store. How are you doing?"

"I'd be doing better if I didn't have to work," I said.

Ray laughed. "Wouldn't we all? You stocking shelves? I'll get you a case."

There were a few customers in the store. I thought my bandaged arm stuck out like a neon sign, but nobody seemed to notice me. Ray gave me a case of peanut butter and I set to work. I didn't have a problem opening the carton. It was heavy enough to tear just by pulling on a flap. There was no price change, but getting the new jars marked and on the shelf seemed to take forever. I must have picked up jars two at a time before.

"Hey, Norm!" Leon looked through the screen door. It seemed like the Fourth of July again. I had a few seconds of thinking it all had been a terrible dream, but when I saw my bandage, that awful heavy feeling came back. I went out to see Leon. Dad wouldn't yell at me in front of customers—not after what had happened.

"They got you working already?"

"Yeah."

"Can you get off to go to the beach this afternoon?"

"I'm not supposed to get the bandage wet."

"So you'll just go in part way. It's going to be really hot today, Norm."

I could tell that already. The small fan in the store wasn't doing anything except moving the hot, sticky air around. It would feel good to get into the water. "Maybe I'll go," I said. "Come back on your way to the beach."

"Okay. I'll come by about lunchtime," Leon said.

I shook my head and grinned at him. "Yeah, perfect timing."

I went back inside and finished shelving the peanut butter.

The store was pretty crowded, mostly with summer people who came up from New York City to get away from the heat. It seemed funny to think of Lake Carmel as a resort area. It was just home to me, but I could see how people would like it if they lived in the city. There was more open space here in Putnam County, with lots of trees and lakes. The population of our town tripled in the summertime. Usually the mothers brought the kids up for the whole summer and the fathers came up on the weekends.

I was about to ask Ray to get me another case when Dad called. "Norman, come back here and give me a hand."

I almost said I didn't have any hands to spare, but when I saw his face, I kept quiet. He must have realized what he had said, because he couldn't look at me. "It's getting busy. I need you to bag groceries."

The customer was a summer person—a lady I didn't recognize. I pulled out a paper bag, snapped it to open it, and started packing the heavier items in the bottom. I was hoping I could get everything into one bag, but I had to start another. It worked out all right. I was able to slide the bag off the counter and hold it with my left arm without hitting the end of it. The lady looked a little worried about me and offered me a big tip after I loaded the bags into her car. "Thanks, but my father doesn't let me take tips," I said.

"No, I insist," she said, so I thanked her again and pocketed the quarter. My very first job at the store had been taking grocery bags out to customers' cars. I had learned early on that a lot of people would offer a tip twice. Dad never said I had to argue with them about it.

The last customer before lunch asked me how I lost the hand. I was sure everybody else had noticed it. This guy was the only one with enough nerve to say anything about it.

"I got it caught in the meat grinder." I could have said something less shocking like "I had an accident," but if this guy was going to be nosy, I'd give it to him with both barrels.

He winced. "That's really tough. How are you getting along?"

"Okay, I guess." I slid the bags into the back seat. Even though it was none of this guy's business, I thought I might get a good tip if I played it up. "I'll get better with practice. Like baseball. I really want to play again. Got to get a right-handed glove, though. I have to save up the money for it." I didn't like people feeling sorry for me, but I was going for the biggest tip I could get.

The guy got a funny look on his face. "Baseball, huh? Good for you." Then he got into his car and drove off without giving me any tip at all. So much for using the poor, crippled kid act to get money.

Leon brought his bike to a gravel-spitting stop in front of me just before I reached the store entrance. "You ready for lunch?" he asked.

"Sure. Let's get sandwiches." We went back to the meat counter. "Hey, Mom, Leon and I are going to the lake, okay?"

"You finish unloading that order?" she asked.

"Some of it. Dad had me bagging groceries for the last hour."

"You can finish later, then. I suppose you two want sandwiches."

"Yes, please, Mrs. Schmidt," Leon said. "That would be wonderful if it wouldn't be too much trouble." Leon turned extra polite when food was involved.

"Roast beef on pumpernickel with mayo for you, Norm?"

"Yeah, thanks, Mom."

"And salami on marble rye with mustard for you, Leon?"

"That's my favorite, Mrs. Schmidt. Especially the way you make it." Leon was practically drooling. Without Mom, he would have starved to death by now.

She smiled at him and shook her head. She made up the sandwiches and put them in the cardboard trays they used for chopped meat. She plopped a big scoop of macaroni salad on Leon's plate, but none on mine, because she knew I didn't like it. "You wait half an hour after eating before you go in the water, boys."

"Sure, Mom," I said, heading for the door. "Thanks for the lunch."

"Norman, don't forget," Mom called, "you can't get the bandage wet."

"I'm just going wading to cool off. I'll keep my arm out of the water."

Leon had finished half of his sandwich before we got to the top of the stairs. I pulled a couple of cream sodas from the fridge. By the time I changed into my bathing suit, Leon had polished off all his food and was eyeing my sandwich.

"Do you have a tapeworm or something?" I asked.

"I was hungry," Leon said. "I'm a growing boy."

"Yeah, you're going to start growing sideways if you keep packing away food like that."

"Hurry up and eat, Norm, it's hot. I want to get into the water."

"I'll eat on the way."

"On your bike?"

I put my towel around my neck, held the soda against my chest with my left arm, and picked up the sandwich. "No. Let's walk."

"You want me to carry your sandwich?" Leon asked.

"You wish," I said.

We cut across back yards to get to Chauncey Road, then down Dunwoodie to West Lakeshore Drive. It was another quarter mile from there to the beach. It felt good to be out doing something. My arm still had that weird tingly feeling at times, but I could put it out of my mind. I had eaten half of my sandwich and really wanted a drink, but I couldn't hold the sandwich and grab the soda at the same time.

Leon saw my problem and held out his hand. "Give it here. I won't take any. Scout's honor."

We passed the bottle and the sandwich back and forth for the rest of the walk. Leon was good to his word. He didn't snitch a bite or a sip.

The beach was pretty crowded with people I didn't recognize. The summer kids were there with their mothers. Before Leon and I were old enough to go to the beach by ourselves, his mother took us, since my mom had to work at the store. I only knew of a couple other kids whose mothers worked. It bothered me sometimes, but that's the way it was when your family had a business.

Leon took off his sneakers and socks. "Come on, Norm, let's go in."

"It hasn't been half an hour."

He turned and grinned at me. "Yeah, right."

The first time we went in right after eating we were sure we would drown, but nothing happened. From then on we figured it was just one of those things mothers said to keep kids from having too much fun.

As I untied my shoes I wished I had taken Mom's advice about learning to tie the laces. By the time I got down to the edge of the water, Leon was halfway out to the raft.

I started wading in past a couple of little kids who were sitting in the shallow water, pushing a rubber ball back and forth between them while a mother watched them. The blond kid looked up at me. "You gotta boo-boo, mister?" he asked, pointing at my bandage.

"Just mind your own business, Sammy," the mother said.

The kid persisted. "Did you get your hand shot off in the war, mister?"

"Yeah, right, kid," I said. "They send eleven-year-olds off to war every day."

"Sammy!" the mother hissed, pulling him out of the water. "I told you not to talk to him."

I ignored them and kept wading. When the water came up to the waistband of my suit, I stopped. I knew there was a drop-off soon after that, so I just stood there. I folded my arms, trying to keep the bandage hidden.

Leon was out on the raft, talking with Gordie Corrigan from our class. Leon pointed at me and Gordie waved. I turned my back on them. I didn't want Gordie coming over here asking about the accident. He was the nosiest kid in the class and he had a big mouth, too. If I told him anything about my accident, he'd be blabbing about me all over the place—probably already was.

Even though my bottom half was cool, the rest of me was dying in the hot sun. Besides, I felt stupid just standing there, not swimming. Then I felt a splash on my back. It was Leon in an inner tube.

"If you get this bandage wet, you're dead meat," I said.

He pulled the tube over his head. "Get in, Norm. I'll tow you out to the raft."

"Nah, I think I'm going home."

"Home? We just got here."

"I know. I don't feel so good."

"Okay. Let me take the tube back to Gordie and I'll come with you."

"No, you stay. It's a good day for swimming."

"You sure?"

"Yeah, I'm sure."

I dried off and stuffed my feet into my shoes, tucking in the laces. I couldn't explain to Leon why I had to leave. Maybe in a few weeks when I didn't have the bandage, the beach would be fun again. Now it was too hard. I felt uncomfortable, and seeing someone from school made it worse—especially somebody like Gordie Corrigan. I felt tears sting my eyes as I walked home. No matter what Dr. Zeigler thought, this wasn't going to be easy. And now that Mom had turned into a Marine drill sergeant, I couldn't even count on her to make me feel better.

As I reached our store's parking lot, a familiar car pulled in. It was the guy who had stiffed me for a tip.

Maybe he was coming back to give it to me. He got out of the car and motioned for me to come over.

"I'd like to give you something," he said. "What's your name?"

"Norman, sir." I was right. I was getting the tip after all. I waited for him to reach into his pocket, but he pulled something out of the back seat instead.

"Norman, this belonged to my son." He handed me a baseball glove—a right-handed one.

"Wow, thanks! You son doesn't use this anymore?" I didn't care how old I got. I wouldn't want my dad giving away my baseball glove.

The man cleared his throat. "We lost Billy last year. He was killed in Okinawa, just before V-J day."

"I'm really sorry," I said. "You sure you don't want to keep this?"

The man smiled, even though he had tears in his eyes. "No. I think Billy would like you to have it. You start practicing now, hear?"

"I will, sir. This is the nicest thing anybody ever did for me. Thanks a lot!"

The guy got back in his car fast, like he didn't want me to see him cry. I slid my right hand into the glove as he drove off. It was perfectly broken in. I could tell Billy had spent a lot of time oiling it. I thought of how awful it must have been to die so far away from home, and how bad his father felt losing him like that. I had no business feeling sorry for myself.

I couldn't wait to try out the right-handed glove. It was a little big for me, but I'd grow into it soon enough. I ran up to my room and turned on the radio. The timing was perfect because there was a Giants game on for inspiration. I started with the glove on my right hand, then I quickly stuck it under my left arm and pulled it off, leaving my right hand free to catch the ball. After a while I could do it pretty fast, pulling off the glove and catching a phantom ball.

Listening to the radio announcer, I pictured myself playing at the Polo Grounds. "Stan Musial hits a high fly ball to left center field. Giants outfielder Sid Gordon goes back for it. Back, back . . . he makes an over-the-shoulder catch and launches the ball to second for the out!"

Watching myself in the mirror, I was surprised how smooth it looked. If a person didn't know I had a missing hand, they might think I was perfectly normal.

Even though the Giants game wasn't over, I wanted to go outside and try out the glove with a real ball. This time I took out a baseball instead of a tennis ball and threw it against the wall. That was where my great technique fell apart. It was one thing to pull off the glove to throw the ball. It was something altogether different to throw the ball against the wall and get my hand into the glove fast enough to catch it. The ball got past me while I was fumbling with the glove.

I finally tried putting the glove on the end of my stump so the mitt was partly held open instead of being squished under my arm. That way I could slip my hand up into it, and I was actually fast enough to catch one of the balls. I had to stop doing that, though, because I still couldn't stand having anything touch the end of my stump. The sharp tingling sensation gave me the creeps.

I sat down on one of the boxes for collecting bottles and thought about being in a real game. I would be constantly taking off and putting on the glove through the whole game. Other kids didn't have to think about that because they used one hand for catching and the other hand for throwing. For me, there was no such thing as the "other" hand.

I had been so dumb to think a right-handed glove was the magical answer to my problems. Nothing was the same anymore. Everything I tried to do was twice as hard as before. And the thing I wanted to do most— the thing I loved more than anything—was impossible. Leon was right. The whole idea of me playing baseball was stupid. I threw the glove across the back yard.

I started around to the front of the building, but as I walked through the parking lot, I remembered the face of the man who gave me the glove. He thought he was doing me a big favor. I couldn't just leave the glove outside to get rained on. I ran back and got it, took it up to my room, and tossed it on the floor of my closet. I closed the door of my room so nobody could hear me, then flopped down on my bed and cried. I didn't like being a sissy, but I couldn't help it. My dream of being a baseball player was over.

After I quit bawling, I thought about the guy— Billy—who had owned the baseball glove, so I pulled it out and put it on top of my dresser. It didn't mean I was going to play baseball anymore, but the glove deserved better than a closet floor.

It also deserved a better owner than me.

Chapter 7

The next Thursday, I woke up early because Mom and Dad were talking loudly in the kitchen.

"I'll get Norm," Mom said. "You know he loves to go to Stamford with you to get the meat and produce. You haven't taken him since the accident."

"Leave him alone," Dad said. "He needs his sleep so he can get better."

"He can sleep anytime. What he needs is to spend time with his father."

I opened my bedroom door. "I'm up. I want to go along, Dad."

"I'm almost out the door," Dad said. "You're not even dressed."

"I'll be fast!" I ran into my room, grabbed the clothes I had worn the day before, and pulled them on. I hopped out into the kitchen still yanking up my second sock, holding my shoes under my arm.

"Sit!" Mom said. She shoved my shoes onto my feet and tied the laces. "Go! Your father's already in the station wagon."

I was still stupid from sleep as I ran across the parking lot, but it felt good to be going to Stamford with Dad again in our old Chevy woody station wagon. Dad bought it for the store right after the war ended. The wooden posts by the back windows had been rotted out, but Dad had a guy put in new wood, so you couldn't tell it had been in bad shape. It ran great, which was more than you could say for our family car.

It was still dark as we headed down Route 52. I settled into my seat and dozed off for a while. Then the jostling of the winding road woke me up just as we were coming into Pound Ridge. That was my favorite part of the ride because there were a whole bunch of mansions in that section—real fancy houses with iron gates in front. I liked to imagine who lived in those houses and make up stories about them in my head. Not too long after that, we crossed the Connecticut state line and made a right turn onto a busier highway. First we passed a lot of ordinary houses, then businesses, until we came into Stamford.

Dad and I always had breakfast at a diner down in the warehouse district. He ordered our usual breakfast—scrambled eggs, toast, and sausage, with coffee for him and milk for me. At home I always had a little bit of coffee with a lot of milk in it, but you couldn't get it that way in a restaurant. When the waitress came back to warm up Dad's coffee, he asked her to pour a little into my half-empty glass of milk. Other than that, Dad didn't have much to say. He just concentrated on eating.

The diner was always the highlight of the Stamford trip for me. I looked around and recognized people

I'd seen before, who probably ate there every day. I liked to guess what they did from what they were wearing. Some of them had the white jackets from the meat wholesaler, some looked like farmers who brought in their produce, and there were others I figured must have been delivery-truck drivers. They all seemed to know one another and yelled back and forth across the tables. Between the clatter of dishes and the shouting, Dad and I couldn't have carried on a conversation anyway.

We always went to the meat wholesaler first, because Dad never knew how much they'd let him buy. Even though meat wasn't rationed anymore, it was still pretty scarce. Then whatever room we had left in the back of the station wagon, we'd fill up with produce. We backed up to the meat loading dock and climbed the steps to the platform. Joe, the main butcher, came over to meet us. "Hey, Walter, how you doing?"

"Can't complain," Dad said.

Joe looked at me. "How about you, Norm? I was sorry to hear about your accident."

"I'm okay," I said. I was surprised they knew about me all the way down here. Had Dad told them? If he did, he was pretty anxious to change the subject.

"We're in a hurry, Joe. I need a side of beef and a half side of pork."

The two of them headed for the cooler, leaving me behind. There was a lot going on, so I didn't mind. A bunch of guys in white jackets pushed around big hunks of meat on hooks that were attached to an overhead rail. They moved the meat to the scales, then out to the loading dock to be put on their delivery trucks. Dad could have had the meat delivered to our store, but he liked to pick out the cuts he wanted instead of taking what they gave him. I know he argued with them about the price, because I could see him now, shaking his head and pointing to another side of beef next to the one Joe wanted him to take. Then Joe pushed the beef over to a big block and chopped off some pieces before Dad would let him weigh it.

The delivery trucks were tall, so the meat came out on the rail at just the right height to be loaded. With us, they had to lift the side of beef off the hook to get it down to the station wagon. Dad always brought clean butcher's aprons to wrap around the meat before they shoved it into the back of the car.

From there we drove about a block to the produce warehouse. It was a big open room loaded with crates of fruits and vegetables. Dad went around thumping on melons, sniffing peppers, and checking the tomatoes all the way to the bottom of the crate. "You have to make sure they're all ripe but not rotten," he told me. After he paid for the order, everything was loaded into the station wagon, and we headed for home.

Dad was in a good mood now. We watched the cars going by on the other side of the road, looking for postwar models, "Are you going to get a new family car this year, Dad?"

"I'll have to. Your mother has been complaining about the old one stalling all the time, and the garage can't get the parts to fix it. I'd like to find one that runs as well as this car."

Dad used to trade in our car every five years, which he would have done in 1942, only that was when the auto plants started making tanks and army trucks instead of cars. They hadn't been making any new parts, either, and all the rubber for tires went to the war effort.

"We won't have to get a station wagon, will we?"

"What's wrong with station wagons?"

"Once you start hauling meat around in them, they don't smell so hot."

"We don't need a big car for the family. I'll probably get a two-door coupe." He looked over and smiled. "Don't worry, I won't be lugging meat in it."

"Do we have to get black, or could it be something snazzy like red?"

Dad laughed. "You want a snazzy car, do you? How about blue? We'll work our way up to red."

"Blue is good," I said. "Do you think I'll be able to drive someday? They let people with one hand drive, don't they?"

Dad stopped smiling. "It's a long time before you can drive. It's way too soon to start worrying about that."

I should have known better than to mention the hand. Every time I brought it up, Dad got upset.

We were going down Route 22 outside of Katonah when I saw something that could put Dad back into a good mood. "Look up ahead. They've put in new Burma Shave signs." Dad and I loved reading those when we were out for a ride. As a matter of fact, Burma Shaves made me want to learn to read in the first place, so I could call out the punch line before anybody else in the car. They were always good for a laugh. There were five signs spaced along the edge of the road, so you could read only one at a time.

When we got close enough, I read, "'Don't stick your elbow . . . out too far . . . or it may go home . . . in another car! . . . Burma Shave.' Boy, that's a good one, huh, Dad? I'll have to remember it for Mom. Don't stick your elbow . . ."

Dad pounded his palm on the steering wheel. "That's not funny, Norm. You don't need to repeat it. Why would they have a sign like that?"

It took me a minute to realize why he was upset. Without thinking, I'd gone and reminded him about my accident all over again.

The following Wednesday morning, Mom told me we were going to Danbury to buy shoes for school, since they weren't rationed anymore. Boy, was I excited about that. Leather had been in short supply for the past few years, since most of it went to making army boots. I had outgrown three pairs of shoes since the war started, so I kept getting the hand-me-downs from my older cousin, Fred. It was bad enough wearing somebody else's stuff, but Fred had the smelliest feet in the world. Even after I scrubbed out the insides with an old toothbrush and Bon Ami Cleanser, they still smelled like rotten eggs. I couldn't wait to toss out those shoes for good.

We stopped in the store so Mom could get money from the cash register. I grabbed a Hershey Bar for the road and followed Mom out to the car.

After she stalled twice at stop signs, I handed her a piece of my Hershey Bar to make her feel better. "Dad says we're getting a new car. I can't wait to see the new models. I bet they'll be beauties."

Mom popped the chocolate into her mouth. "I don't care about beauty. I just want something that will get me where I need to go."

I cared, though. Ever since we heard the auto plants were going to start making passenger cars again, I'd been sketching my idea of what they should look like. I drew the hood and fenders stretched out to points, so my cars looked like they were going fifty miles an hour when they were standing still. I couldn't wait to see if my predictions were right. I figured if the car companies had to change all the assembly lines anyway, they might as well do something fantastic.

When we got into Danbury, Mom found a parking space near the Buster Brown shoe store. Right away I saw a pair of shoes where the laces slipped onto hooks instead of going through holes. I figured you could just slide the laces off the hooks without untying them and lace them up the same way. Mom could tie a triple knot so I could take them off and on without help.

"You sure you want these?" Mom asked. "They look like army boots."

"I think they're hep." I wasn't going to let on about the shoe tying. It wasn't that I hadn't tried. I had, alone in my room at night, but nothing worked.

A salesman came over to us. "Looking for something for school, are we?"

I handed him the shoe. "I'd like to try these."

"All righty, then. Let's see what size you are." He pulled out this metal thing with measurements printed on it. I had to stand while he moved the little sliders to the end of my toes. The one on the side for the width tickled.

The clerk brought a pair in my size. He laced them up. "There you go, young man. Now if you'll step up to our new Shoe Fluoroscope, we'll see how those shoes fit your feet."

The machine was a rectangular wooden box with an opening for your feet. The top had three viewing ports. There was a short one for me and a couple of longer ones that Mom and the salesman looked into. I pressed my forehead to the viewer and saw a pair of greenish skeleton feet with the dark outline of a shoe. I thought it was a fake until I wiggled my toes and the skeleton moved.

"That's right," the salesman said. "Move those toes around a little, son. See how much room he has in there, Mother?"

"Yes, they look roomy enough. He's growing like a weed."

The salesman turned off the machine and the skeleton feet disappeared. "So, shall I wrap these up, or do you want to wear them home?"

"I'm not sure," I said. "Maybe I should try some others." I didn't need to worry about tying laces, because the salesman would do that. I walked around the store, pointing to shoes. "I like those, and those, and the ones in the top row."

The salesman picked up the samples and went

into the back room. By the time he came out, I had picked out four more shoes to try.

Mom looked at her watch. "We can't stay here all day, Norman. I have another errand to run in Danbury before we head home."

"Dad always says you should look at all the possibilities before you buy something, Mom."

"That's for big things like cars. Shoes are shoes. If they fit, you buy."

The salesman was back with a pile of shoeboxes. He tied the first pair on my feet—ugly brown oxfords I wouldn't wear to the hog show at the fair. "These have wonderful arch support," he said.

I nodded, trying to look serious, then made a beeline for the X-ray machine. When he turned it on, I pointed the skeleton feet out like when Ellie did her ballet exercises. Then I made them pigeon-toed. Then I swiveled them back and forth like a skeleton dance. This thing would be great for Halloween.

The salesman looked up from his viewing port. "I can't tell how they fit if you move around like that, son."

"I'm just trying to see how they'll be in real life. Sometimes I walk funny."

Mom wasn't checking out my feet in the machine this time. She just sat in her chair and gave me one of her looks. I could tell I'd better watch myself or I'd be walking funny for real after we got out of there.

"I need to try the others," I said. "These don't feel right."

The next ones were saddle shoes. Mom picked one up. "This looks like a girl's shoe."

"Nuh-uh. Guys wear them, too," I said.

Mom just raised her eyebrows and sighed.

The salesman really cramped my style in the X-ray machine this time. "Just wiggle the toes, son. Don't move your feet."

I tried on the next two pairs of shoes and was going to send the guy out to get the others, but Mom was giving me the look again. The last pair was a dark reddish brown color called "oxblood." I knew that from stocking the shelf of shoe polish in the store. Perfect name for the son of a butcher to wear, but ugly shoes.

"Nice fit here, Mother. Do you want to have a look-see?"

Mom didn't get up—just shook her head and waved him away. "Decide which pair, Norman, and be quick about it."

"Okay, the first ones," I said.

The salesman smiled, but only his lips looked happy. His eyes were telling me to go jump in a lake.

As we were leaving town, Mom pulled into the A&P parking lot. "Why are we stopping here?" I asked.

"Your father wants me to pick up some mint jelly for the store."

"That's silly. Why would you buy it from another store instead of getting a regular order?"

"Lots of small stores do this," Mom said. "If we get it from a distributor, we'll have to buy a full case. Besides, A&P sells it for less than we can buy it wholesale. They're a big chain, so they order huge amounts and get a good price break. We don't sell many. A dozen will last us for six months."

I had been in the A&P a couple of times before when

Dad was checking out the competition. It always amazed me how huge the store was—about ten times bigger than Dad's. The shelves were farther apart than ours so it seemed less crowded. The customers pushed carts around instead of carrying baskets like we had. I couldn't imagine stocking all of those shelves, though. I noticed there were no young kids working there. The guy restocking the cereal aisle had to be about fifty. The candy display was kid heaven—every kind ever invented.

The meat counter stretched all the way across the back with three butchers cutting meat. You had to take a number to be waited on. Dad always said his meat was better than theirs, but this looked pretty good to me.

"Hey, Mom, look at the price for canned beets. That's half of what we charge. You want to get some?"

Mom picked up a can. "We can't sell these. They have an A&P label."

We found the mint jelly and Mom loaded up.

"I don't get why people buy stuff from us if they can get it so much cheaper here," I said.

"Convenience, mostly. They don't want to drive all the way to Danbury just to pick up a few things. And your father has a good reputation as a butcher. He caters to his customers, and people are willing to pay more for the extra service."

When we got to the checkout, Mom put the jars on the counter. The cashier raised her eyebrows. "Must be having one big roast lamb to need all this mint jelly," she said.

Mom just smiled but didn't tell her we were going

to sell it in our store. I think the girl knew, though. She cracked the gum she was chewing and said it again. "Yes, sir, that must be one mighty big roast." She put the jars in two bags, rang up the sale, and pushed the bags toward me. I wrapped my right arm around one of the bags, picked it up, and started for the door.

"Hey, kid, come back here," the cashier called out.

I turned and went back. "What's the matter?"

She leaned on the counter. "What's the matter with *you*? You're a big strong boy. Pick up this other bag for your mother."

I don't know what came over me. Maybe it was because I didn't like this girl's attitude. Anyway, instead of keeping my left arm out of sight the way I usually did, I held it up in front of her face. "What am I supposed to pick it up with?"

"Omigosh!" she said. "I'm so sorry! I didn't know. I didn't mean to . . ."

Mom picked up the other bag. "Don't worry about it. You didn't do anything wrong."

The cashier was practically in tears. "I just feel so awful. If I had known, I would never have said such a hurtful thing."

Mom gave me a shove toward the door. "There's no harm done."

I was laughing as we walked across the parking lot. "Boy, did you see her face? She was practically bawling."

I was still laughing when we got into the car. Then I realized Mom wasn't laughing with me. She had both hands on the steering wheel and was staring straight ahead. "I don't ever want you to do that again."

"Do what?"

Mom spoke so quietly, it was hard to hear her. "I don't ever want you to use your disability to hurt someone."

"But she was asking for it. She was making fun of you for buying all that mint jelly."

Mom turned to look at me. "Listen, some people are going to be uncomfortable around you at first. You need to go out of your way to put them at ease. You deliberately embarrassed that girl."

"So because I lost my hand, I have to make sure people don't feel bad about it? That's not fair."

Mom turned the key in the ignition. "Maybe not, Norman, but it's as fair as it's going to get."

Chapter 8

The summer flew by even faster than usual. Maybe it was because I was dreading school more than ever. The only kid from school I had seen all summer was Leon. When we ran into kids from our class, I usually made an excuse not to talk with them. I didn't want people feeling sorry for me, and I really didn't want to tell people about my accident.

I was sitting at the dining-room table one afternoon, drawing cars, when Mom came up from the store and sat beside me. "Why aren't you outside?"

"I don't feel like getting out."

"Have some friends over, then. How about some of the boys from your scout troop?"

I erased the hood ornament on my car for the tenth time. "I'll see them when school starts. That's soon enough."

"You worried about what they'll say when they see you?"

I shook my head. I wasn't worried about what kids would say. I was worried about what they *wouldn't* say, except behind my back.

Mom slipped off her shoes and rubbed her feet. They always hurt because she had to stand long hours in the store. "Seems to me it would be easier to see a few people before you go back, so it isn't facing everybody at once."

She was right. I could picture walking in and having the whole school standing around me in a big circle—like a game of dodgeball and I was "it."

Mom sighed. "I know one thing. If we don't cut off that dirty bandage, you won't have a problem avoiding people, because nobody will get near you."

"I go to see Dr. Zeigler in a couple of days. He'll give me a new one."

"Last time you were there, he said I could cut the bandage off in a couple of weeks. That was three weeks ago."

"Well, he was wrong! It's my arm. I guess I know whether it needs to be bandaged or not." I gathered my drawing stuff and went to my room. It wasn't long before I heard Leon yelling from the bottom of the stairs.

"Come on up," Mom called. "Maybe you can get Norm to go outside."

"I've *been* outside," I said.

Leon came into my room and picked up my drawing of the car. "That's pretty good. Only I bet the new cars won't even look like cars. They'll run on rails instead of tires."

"That's called a train, stupid," I said, grabbing back my drawing.

"Naw, not regular train tracks. They'll be rails up in the air."

"So how do you get your car up there?"

"Like this. Give me your pencil." Leon turned my paper over and started drawing. "They'll have entry ports every couple of miles, see? You'll drive into one and the door will close behind you. Then you and your car will be whooshed up to the rail, like on an elevator, only faster."

"Okay, hotshot, if you need roads to get to the entry ports, what's the sense of having the rails? Why not just drive on the roads?"

"Traffic jams, that's why. This isn't for places like Lake Carmel. You ever been down by Yonkers during rush hour? The roads are so crowded you can't move. This would take care of that. See how most of the cars are up here? They can't run into each other because it's all electrically timed to keep them apart."

He had drawn a picture of what looked like a bunch of peanuts lined up on a string with little squares down below. Leon couldn't draw worth beans, but I had to admit he had a good imagination. He could be an inventor someday, but he'd have to get somebody to draw his inventions for him or nobody would know what he was talking about.

I took back the paper and added pointy fenders to his cars. "Yeah, that's good," he said.

I turned the drawing with my left arm to get a better angle, and a strip of loose adhesive stuck to the paper. "Hey, what's with the bandage, Norm? That thing is disgusting. Can't you take it off?"

"You been talking to my mother? She put you up to saying that?"

"No. Look at the thing. Why do you need it? It's practically falling off."

"Why is everybody so worked up about my bandage? It'll come off when it falls off."

Mom took me to my doctor's appointment a couple of days later. She stayed in the waiting room and let me go in by myself. That was one of the nice things about Mom. She wasn't nosy.

The office was busy, so I had to wait quite awhile in the little room for the doctor to come in. I almost fell asleep on the table. Then I heard the door open.

"Hey, Norman. Good to see you. How are you doing?"

"Okay, Dr. Zeigler."

"I thought this bandage would be off by now." He pulled some blunt scissors out of a drawer. I looked away as he cut through the bandage. I could feel him turning my arm to look at the end where the stitches had been. "You healed very nicely, Norm. You should be able to do just about anything you want, now. The incision isn't tender anymore, is it?"

"Not unless I hit it on something. The weird thing is that sometimes it feels like my hand is still there."

"That's phantom pain. With some people it goes away fairly soon. Others have it for years."

"If I don't think about it, it's not so bad."

"That's good. How's the baseball going?"

"Not so good. I'm still trying to figure out how to catch with the glove, then get rid of it to throw."

Dr. Zeigler pulled a newspaper clipping out of his desk drawer. "I think this might help you with that. Remember I told you about Pete Gray?"

"Yeah, the one-handed outfielder for the Browns."

"Right. This tells about him. It even describes how he catches and throws."

I studied the picture of Pete Gray. His baseball mitt was tucked under his right arm almost all the way up to his armpit. "Wow, he hardly has any arm at all."

"That's right. His amputation is just a few inches below the shoulder. You still have your elbow and your entire forearm, so you have much more to work with. You should be able to brace your stump against the bat when you swing."

There was that word again. Stump. Only now that we were talking about how I could use it, it didn't sound so bad. "Okay, I'll try that. I've only been practicing throwing and catching so far. Can I keep this?"

"I've been saving it for you, Norm." He patted me on the back. "I don't need to see you again unless you run into problems, but call me once in a while and let me know how you're doing, all right?"

"Sure, Dr. Zeigler."

He got up and headed for the door.

"Aren't you going to put on a new bandage?" I asked.

"You don't need it, Norm."

"Well, what if I'm playing baseball? It wouldn't be good to get the end of my . . . my stump dirty, would it? I mean, couldn't germs get in there?"

Dr. Zeigler laughed. "Norman, you were carrying around enough germs on that old bandage to start an epidemic. Besides, you can wash your stump with ordinary soap and water. It's covered with skin, you know. You don't have to send it out to be dry-cleaned."

"Okay, but maybe just in case I bump it."

"You're going to bump into things every day. And if you hit it just right it's going to hurt like the devil, but a bandage isn't going to help that."

"Maybe a little bandage?" I asked. "Just to cover the end?"

Dr. Zeigler came back and sat down. "What's going on, Norm? You don't want people to see your stump?"

I shrugged. It was more that I didn't want to see it myself, but I wasn't going to tell him that.

"You're not using the bandage to make people feel sorry for you, are you?"

"No! I hate that."

"Is it so you can get out of doing things? Chores around the house?"

"Are you kidding? My mother made me take out the garbage the first night I was home from the hospital."

Dr. Zeigler laughed. "That's good. She took my little lecture seriously."

"What did you say to her?"

"I said to take you home and not do a thing for you."

Well, that explained a lot. "I think she took you too seriously," I said. "You turned her into a monster."

He laughed again. "Boys raised by monsters turn out to be strong." When he noticed I wasn't laughing, he stopped smiling. "Your mother is doing exactly the right thing, Norm. Now, about the bandage, how about I put a small one just over the end of the stump? You can take it off when you feel ready. Try to make that soon, all right? School starts in a couple of weeks, so it should be off before then."

"Okay," I said. But I was lying.

I read the Pete Gray article ten times in the car on the way home. I had been ready to give up on baseball, but if this guy could play with just a few inches of arm, there was no reason I couldn't do it just missing a hand.

The article said Pete caught the ball with the glove directly in front of him about shoulder high, then rolled the glove and ball across his chest from left to right. This would separate the ball from the glove, leaving the glove under his right arm and the ball in his left hand.

Okay, so I would have to reverse that, rolling the glove and ball across my chest from right to left, so the ball would end up in my right hand. The article even explained how Gray fielded grounders, letting the ball bounce off his glove about knee high in front of him. Then he'd flip off the glove and grab the ball while it was still in the air. Boy, I wish I'd seen that. I couldn't believe how lucky I was to have this article. I might have worked for weeks before I figured out how to do this stuff. Now I had it all laid out for me.

It sounded easy when I read about it, but actually doing it was tricky. I took the article outside and read it a couple more times to get the picture in my head. Then I put the glove under my left arm and threw the ball against the wall. Right away, I realized I had the same problem as before. I couldn't practice Pete Gray's technique of getting rid of the glove if I couldn't get it on my hand in the first place. The glove was squeezed shut under my arm, so when I tried to plunge my hand into the opening, it took too many tries and the ball got by me.

I decided to keep practicing, even though part of my brain was telling me, "If you keep doing something that doesn't work, all you're learning is how to do it wrong." But I kept going, because if I quit, I'd never learn anything.

I threw the ball for about an hour, then as I started to get tired, something happened. I wasn't holding the glove so tight under my arm anymore. It was resting in the crook of my elbow, so the glove wasn't being squeezed. Without thinking, I shoved my hand into the opening and brought the glove around in time to catch the ball. Then, I grabbed the glove with my elbow again, took the ball out with my right hand, and threw it. It worked like a charm.

I was on to something. I wasn't even tired anymore. I just kept trying it over and over. I still dropped some, but pretty soon I got into the rhythm of it, and I was catching more than I dropped. I had just solved two problems at once. I didn't need to use Pete Gray's method of getting rid of the glove. He had to do that "rolling across the chest" thing because he just had a little bit of arm below his shoulder. I had an elbow that could work almost like another hand. I could grab things in the crook of my elbow and hold them pretty tight. I wasn't touching anything to the end of my stump, so I didn't get that tingly pain.

I tried it hundreds of times over the next few days. I still dropped the ball, but I caught it often enough to know that someday I'd do it every time.

Batting practice was another problem. I had to hold the bat under my left arm, throw the ball against the wall, then grab the bat in my right hand and swing. Most of the time I missed. That was one thing I really needed to practice with another person. It couldn't be Leon, though. Every time he saw me practicing, he tried to discourage me, so I only did it when he wasn't around. I knew he didn't want to see me get shot down by failing, but he didn't realize he was shooting me down himself by not believing in me.

I gave up on the batting and worked on throwing and catching. My bandage was turning gray and hanging in little shreds around the edges from the abuse it took.

About a week before school started, I was throwing and catching against the wall when Leon pulled into the parking lot on his bike. I let the ball roll under some bushes. I didn't have time to hide the glove, so I just held it behind my back.

He put down the kickstand and came over. "Whatcha got?"

"Nothing."

"Yeah, right." He tried to peek over my shoulder. "You got something to eat. What is it? A sandwich? Doughnut?"

"No. I told you I don't have anything."

"We'll see about that." He tackled me, reached behind, and came up with the glove.

"Aw, Norm, you're not on that baseball kick again, are you?"

"None of your beeswax." I grabbed the glove, but I hadn't noticed that a strip of adhesive from my bandage was stuck to it. As I yanked, I felt the bandage slip off. I dropped the glove and walked away from Leon. I couldn't look at my stump.

"Where are you going?" Leon called after me.

"No place. Just leave me alone." I went around behind the garage where nobody could see me. I sat on the ground and leaned back against the garage wall. Then I took a deep breath and looked at my stump. It's hard to explain, but as long as the bandage was on, I didn't get the full picture about having no hand. Now here it was, naked except for the bright orange stain from the Mercurochrome that Dr. Zeigler had put on it and the dark strip of dirt where the edge of the bandage had been. My arm looked normal up by the elbow, then when it got to my wrist, it just rounded off and stopped. I looked at the end of my stump, expecting to see a Frankenstein scar, but you could barely see where the stitches had been.

"You okay?" Leon was peeking around the side of the garage.

"Yeah, I guess so."

Leon came over and sat next to me. "Good thing orange is your favorite color."

"I think it'll wash off," I said.

"That doesn't look bad at all, Norm. It's about time that stupid bandage came off."

"Yeah," I said, feeling a weight lift from my shoulders. "It is."

Chapter 9

*T*he day I had been dreading finally arrived. The first day of school had always seemed like being sent to prison for having too much fun over the summer, but this year it felt more like an execution.

I was standing outside the store waiting for the bus when Dad came out. "All ready for school, Norman?"

"As ready as I ever am."

Dad patted my back. "Everything is going to be fine. Just act like nothing happened, you know? Just go ahead like it's a normal day."

I know Dad wanted to make me feel better, but his words had the opposite effect on me. I hadn't really been thinking that much about my hand lately. Ever since the bandage came off, I was using my stump more and more, so it was beginning to feel almost natural. I hadn't even put on a long-sleeved shirt this morning to cover it up. But now, after Dad's pep talk, I was worried about facing all those kids who had heard about my accident and wanted to see how much of a freak I was. And even worse, what if some of the kids hadn't heard about it? They'd be shocked when they saw me.

I glanced through the store window at the clock, to see if I had time to change into a long-sleeved shirt. But when I looked down the road, I saw the big yellow shape of the school bus come over the top of the hill.

Dad gave me another pat on the back. "Remember, just pretend nothing's different."

When I got on the bus, I felt as if everybody was staring at my stump. Thanks a bunch, Dad. At least most of the Mercurochrome stain had faded so it wasn't bright orange anymore.

I picked a window seat on the left side near the back. That way my stump wouldn't be facing the aisle. I was one of the first stops on the bus, which meant I had almost an hour's ride to school, even though we could get there in twenty minutes by driving direct. Some kids complained about the long ride, but I never had minded it. I always watched out the window as we wound through farmland on back roads. It gave me time to daydream, not that I didn't always find plenty of time for that in school.

Leon lived only two blocks away, but that was just far enough for us to be on different bus routes. He got to school in half the time that my bus took.

A bunch of younger girls got on at the next stop. I thought I heard one of them say "That's him" as they passed me. I should have sat all the way in the back so nobody would walk by my seat. I heard them whispering behind me, and I felt my ears burning red. After that, I didn't look at anybody who got on. Well, not directly, but I could see them out of the corner of my eye. Was it my imagination, or were they all whispering about me?

I tried to look busy opening my pencil box. I had great pencils this year—red, blue, and green ones with metallic paint and colored erasers to match. Then I realized I had forgotten to get Dad to sharpen them for me in the back room of the store. How could I do that in school? Maybe if I pressed on the eraser end with my stump it would keep the pencil from spinning around when I cranked it. But what if that didn't work? Most teachers had the pencil sharpener at the front of the room where everybody would see me.

Wait! Leon would do it for me. We had the same teacher—Miss Bean in room 225. We had compared notes when we got our class assignment cards in the mail in August. Phyllis said Miss Bean was one of the nicest and easiest teachers in the school. I had really lucked out this year.

We pulled up by Cressman's farm and Ronnie and Charlie got on. Ronnie was in my class and my scout troop. I didn't look up, but he came and sat next to me anyway. "Hi, Norm."

Ronnie was a big kid, so I had to move over to make room for him, but I kept looking out of the window. "Hi, Ronnie."

I could see his reflection leaning forward in his seat. He was trying to see my left arm. I kept it pressed close to the side of the bus, out of his view.

"I heard about what happened to you this summer, Norm. You doing okay now?"

I shrugged. I wasn't going to get into a discussion with Ronnie about my accident.

But Ronnie wouldn't let it go. "My cousin Arnie lost his arm a few years ago when he got it caught in the hay baler. Ripped it clean off up to here." Ronnie made some chopping motions halfway between his elbow and shoulder. I felt an explosion of sharp tingles where my hand should be. I took a deep breath and swallowed.

"He's okay now, though," Ronnie said. "They got him one of those hooks and he can do just about anything he wants. He can even light a cigarette with it."

I nodded. Why was lighting a cigarette such a big deal for these people who teach you how to use a hook? Seemed to me cutting a steak would be more useful. Or tying your shoes, for Pete's sake. I glanced down at my new shoes. I had Mom tie them with triple knots a couple of days ago so I could practice taking the laces on and off the fasteners. So far, it was working really well. I had thought about squeezing some airplane glue into the knots to make sure they didn't come loose, but decided it would look odd. Besides, as the laces stretched I'd have to have the knots tied tighter.

"So where was yours cut off?" Ronnie asked.

He obviously wasn't going to give up. "In my father's meat market."

"I know that. I mean where on your arm?"

He was making those darn chopping motions again, going up and down his arm. Each chop put a little shock through my hand.

To stop him, I pointed to his wrist. "About here," I said.

"Yeah? Lemme see."

Here I go, I thought. Even if I tried to hide my

stump, kids were going to ask to see it. Then they'd probably puke, or the girls would make a face and say, "Eeeuw!" Maybe I should just stand up in the bus and yell, "Everybody who wants to see an arm with no hand on it can look right now." Better yet, I could charge kids a nickel to see it. Maybe even more. They charged a quarter for the freak show at the fair.

"Norm?" Ronnie said. "Lemme see it."

I pulled my stump out from its hiding place and waited for the reaction.

"That's not bad at all, Norm. I bet you'll do a lot better than Arnie."

"Yeah, I'll be lighting cigarettes in no time."

"No kidding. You smoke?"

"No, do you?"

He shook his head and we both laughed.

I felt better after that. If my stump didn't creep Ronnie out, maybe it wouldn't bother most other kids, either. Of course, Ronnie wasn't your usual kid. He lived on a pig farm. It took a lot to creep him out.

When we got to school, I headed for room 225. Leon was already in the classroom. "Hey, Norm, I saved you a seat." It was in the back row. Perfect. I did my best daydreaming in back rows. It was by the window, too. Leon knew a good location when he saw one.

I pulled out my pencils. "Hey, Leon," I whispered. "Can you sharpen one of these for me?"

"Sure. Those are really neat. Can I borrow one? I forgot mine."

Leon always "forgot" his school supplies, and I knew he'd be borrowing this pencil until it was worn down to a little nub, but that was okay. Friends were supposed to help each other out.

"I'll take a green one," Leon said. "I know you like red and blue the best."

Leon slipped back into his seat just before the bell rang, handing me two perfectly sharpened pencils—one red and one blue.

Miss Bean started out by having everybody stand along the walls. Then, as she called the roll, she assigned seats in order, calling names from the front of each row to the back. Since Ludewig and Schmidt were so far apart in the alphabet, Leon and I didn't get to sit by each other. Worse yet, I ended up in front, right in plain sight. I was just thankful that I had a teacher who would go easy on me. Otherwise sixth grade could be a complete disaster.

Next, Miss Bean passed out our books and gave us paper covers to put on them. Barbara Sager offered to help me put on my book covers.

"That's nice of you, Barbara," Miss Bean said, "but I think Norman can manage fine on his own. Isn't that right, Norman?"

"Yes, Miss Bean." I was glad she said that. I knew I could do it, because I had to refold grocery bags in the store. Besides, I always liked covering books, making the folds so it fit just right. And then I had that nice blank paper cover just waiting for my drawings. The social studies book was big. I could draw a lot of stuff on that cover.

After lunch, Miss Bean sent us to the auditorium for music. Mr. Margolus, the music teacher, stood on the stage. "Boys and girls, now that you're in sixth grade, you're going to pick out an instrument to play in the band. The school owns all the instruments, so everybody will get one. First, I need to ask if anybody owns an instrument or has an older brother or sister who has an instrument you can use. May I see a show of hands?"

Leon elbowed me. "That would be show of hand, in your case."

"You're just lucky he didn't ask for a show of brains," I whispered.

About a dozen kids raised their hands, and Mr. Margolus had them go up on the stage and tell him what instrument they had. He pointed to where he wanted each one of them to sit.

The rest of us got pretty noisy, so Mr. Margolus had to whistle through his teeth to shut us up. "All right, boys and girls, keep it down. When I call your name, tell me what instrument you'd like to play. Then you'll come up on the stage and I'll put you in the appropriate spot." He started calling out names. Most of the girls wanted clarinets, and the boys wanted trumpets. "We're running out of the clarinets and trumpets, people. Let's hear some bolder choices here. How about the sousaphone and saxophone?"

"What are you going to pick, Norm?" Leon whispered.

"I don't know. Everything I can think of takes two hands."

"Yeah, you're right. You gotta come up with something, though. Everybody has to be in the band. I'm going to choose trombone."

"Why trombone?"

"Trombones have this long slider thing and you can poke the kid in front of you in the rear with it."

"Good reason for picking an instrument," I said.

"It gets even better," Leon whispered. "Your spit builds up inside the trombone when you play, and then you pull this little lever and you can squirt it on someone. Is that the world's coolest instrument, or what?"

"Sounds like a weapon," I said.

Mr. Margolus was pretty excited when Ronnie chose the tuba. "Great choice, Cressman. Great choice!"

"Tubby gets the tuba," somebody behind us snickered.

Just then, Mr. Margolus called Leon's name. "I choose the trombone, sir."

Mr. Margolus smiled. "Another good choice, Ludewig. Not easy to play, but a fine instrument." Leon grinned and headed for the stage.

I had been fine sitting there with Leon, but now that I was alone I was getting worried. What instrument would I have to play?

Carl Oberndorfer, a new kid in school, was called after Leon. He picked the snare drums. That would be fun, but you couldn't use just one drumstick. What if I got stuck with something stupid like a tambourine? We had those in kindergarten. That would be humiliating, especially when the band played in front of the whole school. I'd be up there playing some baby instrument with everybody looking at me.

"Norman Schmidt, are you here?"

The girl in front of me turned around. "Norman, he's been calling you."

I ran up to the stage. I didn't want to be shouting out my problem for the whole sixth grade to hear. "You probably didn't know this, Mr. Margolus, but I only have one hand now. I can't play an instrument."

"Sure you can, Schmidt," he said. "I'm putting you on drums."

"That would be great, but don't you have to use two drumsticks? And I don't think my doctor would want me to—"

"Bass drum, Schmidt. Bass drum. One drumstick, one hand. Just boom, boom, boom. You'll do fine. Go sit by Oberndorfer."

As I walked over to my place, I had a sneaky feeling that Mom had gotten to Mr. Margolus.

Leon gave me a thumbs-up as I passed by him. His chair was behind Evelyn Rednick. He did a little trombone-slide pantomime, aimed right at her rear end. Poor Evelyn had no idea what a miserable year she was in for.

Chapter 10

*F*inally, fifth period came along—gym, my favorite class. I was hoping we'd get to play baseball. Since I'd been practicing every day, I'd been getting pretty good, and I was looking forward to surprising a few people—especially Leon.

Leon and I grabbed our gym clothes from our lockers. "Where are your sneakers, Norm?" he asked.

"I forgot them. It doesn't matter. We'll be outside today."

"Yeah, so that's okay for now, but what are you going to do on a day when it rains? Mr. Locke won't let you wear leather-soled shoes in the gym."

"I just forgot my sneakers, that's all. Quit making such a big deal about it."

Leon gave me a look. "You can't tie your shoe-laces, can you?"

"No, I can't. Now are you happy?"

"Take it easy. I'm just trying to help."

"Some help you are!" I pushed past him and headed for the locker room. Leon was right, though. On a rainy day, I'd have to change into sneakers. And I couldn't just have the sneakers tied at home and wear them to school, because you couldn't wear shoes in the gym that had been worn outside.

Leon caught up with me. "I was trying to say I could tie them for you."

"Just drop it, Leon. I'm going to figure out how to do it myself."

"Okay! Fine!"

We changed into our shorts and T-shirts and went out onto the baseball field. Our gym teacher, Mr. Locke, was the coach for Lake Carmel's team in the summer baseball league. If I could impress him in gym class, I'd have a good chance of making the team when it was time for tryouts.

Mr. Locke picked two kids as captains, then they chose their teams. Leon got picked in the fifth round, but nobody called my name. Even girls were getting picked before me. When it got down to three girls and me, Mr. Locke went over to one of the team captains and whispered something to him. The kid nodded and called my name, but I could tell he wasn't happy about it. If Mr. Locke hadn't said something I probably would have been the last kid called. Nobody wanted a cripple on their team, but I'd show them I was a cripple who could play baseball.

Our team was first up at bat. Since I had been picked second to last, I had a long time to wait. I hadn't practiced batting much, but I used to be pretty good at it, so I figured I'd do all right. I probably wouldn't have to bat in the first inning. I'd have a chance to show my fielding skills first. Leon waved at me from the field, and I waved back.

The pitcher on the other team wasn't very good. Our first six batters made it to first base on balls. Then they changed pitchers, and a couple of kids got singles. I had been daydreaming about making a spectacular catch in right field and lobbing the ball in to second for an out when somebody called my name.

"Hey, Norm! You're up!"

I jumped to my feet and headed for the plate. Mr. Locke handed me the bat. "Just do your best, Norm."

I took a couple of practice swings, but my stump was sort of flailing in the air, and it felt awkward. I rested the side of my stump against the bat and tried again. That was a little better, but I could see everybody staring at me, wondering if I could hit the ball. I nodded to Mr. Locke and he called, "Play ball."

The first one was high and outside, but I was so jumpy, I swung at it.

"Strike one!"

What a stupid move! I had to pay more attention.

I didn't swing at the next pitch, but Mr. Locke called it a strike.

If I didn't shape up, I was going to be the first one in the game to strike out. The next pitch looked good, so I swung at it with all of my strength. This time I connected with the ball. There was a loud crack, and the worst pain I had ever felt shot all the way up to my armpit. I thought I might have broken a bone, but then I recognized the sickening shock I got when I hit my stump. I started blindly running for first base, when I heard Mr. Locke yell, "Foul ball!"

I wanted to run off the field and throw up, but I turned and went back to the batter's box. I was so dizzy, I couldn't tell whether the next ball was high or low, inside or outside. I just swung at it so I could get out of there.

"Strike three! Third out. Change sides." Everybody was getting gloves from the other team as they came off the field. There weren't any right-handed ones.

"Sorry about that, Norm," Mr. Locke said. "I'll have one for you for the next game. You want to try fielding without a glove or sit this one out?"

"Sit out." I could barely talk, and I was fighting to keep back the tears from the throbbing pain and the humiliation of striking out. So much for showing off. I found a spot to sit against the fence away from everybody else. I closed my eyes and took a few deep breaths, but the funny-bone-from-hell feeling was still vibrating through my arm. I could hear the shouts and sounds of the game going on without me.

It would be a lot easier to give up on baseball and just do the stuff I could manage with one hand. So what if Pete Gray could play in the majors with almost no arm? Maybe he was one of those superhumans who could do anything he put his mind to. I could get an excuse from gym from now on. I knew I had made the right decision when nobody noticed that I didn't take my turn at bat in the next inning. It was like I was gone already.

Somehow I managed to get through the school day, even though the pain stayed with me. I noticed some kids avoided looking me in the eye after seeing me flub it in the gym disaster. Leon was the only one who said anything about it. "Big deal. So you struck out. Who hasn't done that? I bet I've struck out a million times."

"I was the only one who struck out today. All the rest of the kids were called out on base."

"You're not trying out for the Giants, Norm. It's just a game. Forget about baseball. It's not gonna work for you anymore."

Even though I had decided the same thing back in gym class, just hearing Leon say that made me want to prove him wrong.

At the end of the day, Miss Bean gave out homework in math, social studies, and science. Three subjects on the first day. I wondered how the heck she got a reputation for being nice.

When the last bell rang, I went up to Miss Bean's desk. "I don't think I can do homework this year, Miss Bean."

She looked up. "And why is that, Norman?"

"Well, you gave assignments in three different books for tonight."

"Yes, I did. And that's a problem because . . ."

"Well, I'll have to take all those books home. They're kind of heavy and I only have one hand." I didn't like having people feel sorry for me, but I'd stoop to playing for sympathy if it would get me out of homework.

Miss Bean smiled at me—that kind of "teacher smile" that lets you know she's on to you. "Oh, I see. You think I should excuse you from doing homework because of that, do you? Having only one hand?"

I had a feeling this wasn't going well, but I forged ahead. "Yes, Miss Bean. I can get a note from home if you need it." I was a lousy liar and I hoped she couldn't see I was bluffing. No way Mom would write me a note, and even if I got up the nerve to try it, my handwriting wasn't good enough to pass for hers.

"Norman, I've been looking at your school record, and I think you can do much better this year than you have in the past."

"Oh, I don't think so," I said. "I've had quite a set-back, you know." I bit my lip and tried to look sad.

"You're a smart boy, Norman. Smart enough to know that this little act of yours isn't making any impression on me. Understand?"

I understood all right. I was beginning to get the picture loud and clear. "Miss Bean, did you talk with my mother by any chance?"

Miss Bean gave me that smile again. "She's a lovely woman, Norman. She came in to see me last week. I know she wouldn't want me to expect anything but the best from you. Your very best effort. And that includes homework."

"Okay, Miss Bean." I could feel the trap closing. From now on, wherever I went, my mother would get there first and mess things up for me. I was doomed. I picked up my books—trying to make them look a lot heavier than they were—and headed for the door.

"Norman."

I turned. "Yes, Miss Bean?" Had it worked? Had she changed her mind?

"That was a very nice try. Admirable, in fact. You might consider joining the drama club this year."

I sighed. "I'll think about that, Miss Bean."

All the way home on the school bus, I thought about how I could practice batting by myself. By the time I reached my stop, I had a plan. I slipped by the store window fast so I wouldn't get stuck working, changed my clothes, and went out back.

My idea was to hang a baseball from a tree limb at the right height to swing at. I got some rope from the garage and tried to wrap it around the ball. It needed to go around in several directions and be tied tight. I could picture just the way I wanted it, but I couldn't do it with one hand. I was about to give up, when Ellie came into the back yard. "What are you doing, Norm?"

"Nothing."

"Yes, you are. You're trying to tie up that baseball."

"Why would I do that?" I didn't want to admit to Ellie that I couldn't.

Ellie shrugged. "How should I know? You have your bat out here. Are you practicing baseball?"

"Yes. I'm trying to."

"Want me to pitch to you?"

"Okay. That might work."

But it didn't work. Ellie had two kinds of balls, which she alternated, either rolling on the ground or flying over my head. Letting her tie up the ball would be much less frustrating than this.

"I'm not a very good pitcher," she said.

"Never mind. Grab that rope." I told her what I needed. She wrapped rope around the ball in several directions and tied it. "I learned square knots in Brownies." It was amazing to see that two hands—

even ones as clumsy as Ellie's—could do things so much easier than I could.

I tossed the rope over a tree limb and pulled until the ball was the right height. "Did you learn slipknots in Brownies?"

Ellie frowned. "I'm not sure."

I talked her through it, then pulled on the rope. It was perfect.

"Thanks, Ellie. Now I can practice."

"You don't want me to pitch any more balls to you?"

"Nope. I'm all set."

Ellie smiled. "Okay. I'll help you whenever you want." I think it made her feel grown-up to help her older brother.

I waited until she left before I started batting. I was afraid to rest my stump against the bat, because I could still feel the tingling from gym, so I let the left arm swing in the air. That worked at first, but when I really clobbered the ball, it came untied. I decided to make the rope go through the ball instead of wrapping around it. I clamped the ball in the vise on my father's workbench, and took out his drill. By leaning my chest against the top knob of the drill to steady it, I could crank with my right hand. It took a while to drill through all the insides and hard core of the ball. Then I poked the rope down through the hole and kept making loop knots until the line couldn't pull up through the ball anymore.

When I hung it back on the limb, I finally had the perfect setup for batting practice. I didn't have any power behind my swing, though. It was hard to tell how far the ball would go if it wasn't attached to the rope, but I was pretty sure I wasn't hitting any homers.

That night at dinner, Ellie was talking nonstop about her new teacher. "Miss Rooney is so bee-yoo-tiful. She has dark hair and the prettiest blue eyes. She was wearing this gorgeous purple dress with high-heeled shoes to match."

"That's fine, Ellie," Mom said. "But what about homework? Do you have anything you need to get done tonight?"

"Oh, no, Mom. Miss Rooney said she didn't want to give us homework the first few nights. She's the nicest teacher in the school."

Dad looked at me. "You're pretty quiet there, Norm. How did your day go?"

"Fine," I said. "Except for the fact that my teacher was supposed to be the nicest one in the school, until Mom went in and ruined her."

"What's this?" Dad asked. "Lucille, you talked with Norman's teacher?"

Mom scraped the leftover mashed potatoes into Knocky's bowl. "Yes, I went in to school last week."

"Well, that's good, Norman. So your mother let your teacher know you might be having a little trouble with things at first. That was a smart thing to do."

"Yeah, that would have been smart. But instead Mom went around telling everybody to be extra hard on me."

Mom was giving me a really dirty look. "I didn't tell

anybody to be hard on you, Norman. I just don't want them making things too easy for you."

"Sounds like the same thing to me," I mumbled.

"That's enough, Norman," Mom said.

That ended the discussion, but later, after Ellie went to bed and I was doing my homework in my room, I could hear Mom and Dad arguing. I pressed my ear to my door. I couldn't make out all the words, but every now and then I could hear my name. Dad was mad at Mom for going to school and turning everybody against me. I hoped he would tell her to go back and set everybody straight. I wasn't sure that would work, though.

After they stopped, Dad came into my room. "You still working on that homework, Norman? It's getting pretty late."

"I'm finished with the science, and I read the chapter for social studies, but I'm having trouble with the math."

Dad pulled the extra chair over to my desk. "Let me take a look at that."

I shoved the book in front of him. "We're supposed to copy these problems out of the book, then solve them. I copied them all, but it's multiplying three place numbers by three place numbers. Like this one—757 times 324. It's hard."

"You know how to do it, though, don't you, Norm?"

"Sure, but I guess I'm just tired. First day of school and all, you know?"

"We'll do it together, then," Dad said. "Seven times four is twenty-eight, carry the two, five times four is twenty, carry the two. . . . You know about carrying, right?"

"Oh, sure, Dad, I do that 'carry the two' stuff all the time. It's just that I'm"—I yawned—"sleepy."

"Give me a clean piece of paper," Dad said. "I'll give you a little help here. Just because you're tired. First day back to school. I don't know why the teacher can't give you a little break."

I was going to remind Dad whose fault it was that Miss Bean didn't give me a little break, but I figured he'd already had that one out with Mom. And from the looks of things, Dad won. Maybe things would be better from now on.

I tried to keep my eyes open while Dad droned on about carrying twos and fives and eight plus seven is fifteen. Every now and then he'd say, "You're following this, aren't you, Norm? Stop me if I'm going too fast."

"I'm right there with you, Dad," I lied. "It's clear as cellophane."

Finally he handed me the sheet of paper. "There, we're finished. Now copy the answers onto your good paper and get yourself some sleep."

"Thanks, Dad. I will."

I had just finished copying Dad's answers and was about to pack up my homework when Mom knocked on my door.

"Norm? Are you awake?"

"Yes, Mom."

She came in. "So you're mad at me for talking with your teachers."

"Who did you talk to besides Miss Bean and Mr. Margolus?"

"That's not important. I just want you to know why I did it."

"I know. It's for my own good. That's what parents always say when they do stuff that hurts their kids."

She sat down on my bed. "Is that what you think? I want to hurt you?"

"It feels like that to me. You never used to be mean."

"I'm mean because I don't want to see my son selling pencils on the sidewalk someday, that's why."

"Pencils! Why would I sell pencils? I can't even sharpen them!"

Mom smiled. "You're trying to cover up with your jokes. Maybe that's a good thing, but you know what I'm talking about."

"Not really."

Mom leaned forward and spoke in a quiet voice. "Everything is going to be harder for you now, Norm, so you have to work twice as much just to stay even with where you were before. I expect you to push yourself, because I won't let you fail. Do you understand?"

"I guess so," I said. Now I felt guilty for letting Dad do my math homework. The paper with Dad's writing on it was sticking out from under my math book. I held my breath, hoping that Mom wouldn't notice it.

She didn't. She kissed me on the forehead. "I'm only doing this because I love you, Norm."

After she left, I stayed awake thinking for a long

time. I had one parent who wanted to make every-thing easier for me, and the other was making my life miserable. As much as I hated to admit it, I had the feeling that Mom might be right.

But that didn't mean I had to agree with her.

Chapter 11

*F*all was the time for Boy Scout meetings to start up again. Most of the guys in my class were in our troop. Leon came over to our house Monday after school to pick me up.

"How come you're not ready, Norm? We're going to be late."

I was trying to roll up my scout neckerchief on my desk. Every time I picked it up to put it on, it came unrolled.

"Here, let me do that. You know what a stickler Mr. Palmer is for having your uniform perfect." Leon rerolled the neckerchief and put it around my neck. "Can you put on the slide and tie the knots yourself?"

"I don't know. I didn't get that far yet."

Leon rolled his eyes. "I'll do it for now, but you can't be going around having other guys do your neckerchief for you."

"I've got it figured out. Once you get the slide on, I'll keep the knots in the ends of the neckerchief and just put it over my head from now on."

"Yeah, I guess that'll work."

We rode our bikes to the patrol meeting at the Grange Hall. We were the last ones there, getting in line just in time for inspection. Leon got points off for his shirt being wrinkled. Mine was wrinkled, too, but Mr. Palmer didn't say anything. I guess Mom hadn't given him her "be tough on Norman" speech.

"We have a Boy Scout Jamboree coming up in three weeks," Mr. Palmer told us. "We need teams to compete in primitive fire building, orienteering, first aid, and knot tying. Pick your event tonight so you have a week to practice before we put the final teams together."

Leon pulled me aside. "Want to do fire building?"

I shrugged. "If it's primitive fire building, you have to strike flint against steel to get the spark. I can't see how I'd do that anymore with one hand."

"We can work as a team. You stack the logs and I'll make the sparks. Besides, building fires is the most fun. Orienteering is that boring stuff with a compass, and first aid is just bandages and splints."

"You're great at knot tying, Leon. You should sign up for that."

"Yeah, but you can't do it, so I won't, either."

When we told Mr. Palmer what we wanted to do, he tried to talk us out of it. "We already have enough boys on the fire-building team. We could use more people for orienteering or knot tying. You did very well with knots last year, Leon."

"I kind of had my heart set on fire building," Leon told him. "So did Norm."

Mr. Palmer handed Leon one of the patrol's flint

and steel sets. "You can gather dead wood and kindling in the grove of trees out back, then lay your fire in the cleared area by the parking lot. Gordon and Buddy are doing a tepee fire, and Bob and Chuck are laying a lean-to. Why don't you two try a log cabin?"

Leon and I started looking for wood. Leon found a thick dead branch right away. "This will make a good base if we cut it in half. Let me use your ax, Norm."

"I can do it," I said.

"You sure? You don't have any hands to spare, you know."

"I can't cut off the hand that's holding the ax."

Leon grinned. "Yeah, I guess you're safe unless you lop off a toe or two." He went to gather more wood while I chopped the log. I started out steadying it with my stump while I cut, but the blows sent that electric shock through me. As I switched to holding the log with my foot, I thought Leon might be right about me losing a few toes. By the time we dragged our stuff out into the clearing, the other guys had their fires laid out and were working on making sparks.

I liked building the log cabin. It seemed like an art project to me. The object was to start with the biggest pieces at the bottom, then crisscross layers of thinner and thinner branches toward the top. That way the smaller stuff would catch easily and keep dropping down, setting the lower layers on fire. When I got it finished it looked like one of those ancient Mayan temples in our social studies book. I almost wished we didn't have to burn it up.

Leon pulled a hunk of tinder out of the fire-building sack. It looked and felt like cotton candy, only it was brown—made out of some kind of fine wood bark. He set it on the ground, then started hitting the steel against the flint to make sparks. At first he couldn't make any sparks at all. I tried to coach him, but he just didn't have the knack or the patience for it. Without thinking, I reached out with both hands to take the flint and steel from him. I could feel how to do it in my hands—even the one that wasn't there.

Leon looked up. "What are you doing, Norm?"

"Nothing. Just hit the flint sharper."

Leon sat back on his heels. "Maybe we should settle for orienteering."

"C'mon, Leon. Give it a few more tries."

Leon sighed and tried again. He got some sparks this time. I leaned close to the tinder and blew, slow and easy, trying to coax one little spark to make the tinder burst into flame. Finally one took. Leon picked up the smoldering tinder in his hands, blowing on it the same way I had. When it was burning steadily, he laid it gently on the twigs at the top of my log cabin. Then I blew on the tinder while Leon kept feeding in small, dry twigs. "We need more twigs, Leon. I'll keep this going while you get some."

We were the only ones who had our fire started. Mr. Palmer would be sorry he tried to talk us out of fire building. I leaned in and blew softly on the top of the log cabin to keep it burning.

A couple minutes later, I heard Leon yell, "Norm! Watch out!"

"What?" That's when I noticed that even though I had pulled back from the fire, my chin was feeling hot—very hot. I looked down to see that the ends of my neckerchief were burning.

Leon tackled me and pushed me flat on the ground, rolling me over on my stomach to smother the flames.

Mr. Palmer came running over. "Norm! Leon! You know I don't allow roughhousing at patrol meetings."

"Sorry, sir," Leon said. "It was my fault."

I didn't want Leon to take the blame for my dumb mistake, but when I started to say something, he yanked me to my feet, turned me around so Mr. Palmer couldn't see my neckerchief, and pretended to be brushing dirt off my back. "I just lost my head there for a minute, sir. It won't happen again."

"It'd better not, Leon, or your father will hear about this. Now get to work. The others already have their fires blazing."

I looked at our fire. After all that work, there wasn't a sign of a flame—just a little charred tinder. So much for being the champ fire builders.

When Mr. Palmer walked away, Leon pulled off my neckerchief.

"What are you doing?"

"Retying the knots to cover the burned parts," he said. "You won't be able to tell anything happened."

"Why did you take the blame for me? Mr. Palmer is always after you about something."

"That's right, so his opinion of me hasn't changed a bit. Now if he found out that you set your own neckerchief on fire, he might be a little upset."

"It was an accident, for Pete's sake!"

Leon finished the knots in my neckerchief. "Yeah, and the meat grinder was an accident, too, if you catch my drift."

"No, I don't. What are you getting at?"

"You're a disaster waiting to happen, Norm. If Palmer knew about this, he'd be watching you like a hawk. He's a real stickler on safety."

Gordie Corrigan came trotting over with a big grin on his face. "Nice fire-building technique you got there, Norm. I must have missed the part in the handbook where it tells you to use your neckerchief as a fire starter. What page is that on, anyway?"

"Buzz off, Gordie," I said.

Gordie grinned. "Good thing Palmer didn't see you going up in flames, Norm. He's already jumpy about you having one hand. You keep this up and he won't let you do anything but sit around and watch the rest of us real scouts."

Leon was making sparks with the flint and steel again. Gordie elbowed him aside and lit our tinder with a Zippo. "Now there's *my* fire starter, suckers. Works every time."

"Cut it out, Gordie," Leon said. "You know we can't use lighters or matches."

"You guys must have the old Middle Ages Handbook. Mine says anybody who goes off into the wilderness with flint and steel to light fires is a moron."

With that he went back to his roaring fire.

School was going better than I had expected. Kids were getting used to seeing me with one hand, so they weren't staring as much. Then, exactly one week after my gym disaster, we went out to play baseball again. As soon as Mr. Locke saw me, he slapped the side of his head. "I knew I forgot to do something. I didn't get that right-handed glove for you, Norm."

"I have one at home, Mr. Locke. Couldn't I just bring that to school?"

"We're not supposed to have kids bring in their own equipment. Don't worry, I'll have the glove next time we play. Your team is batting first."

Even though I had been practicing, when I got up to bat and looked over at Leon, I lost my confidence. I could tell from the expression on his face that he expected me to strike out. The first pitch was a ball, and I didn't swing at it. Same with the next one. Then I hit the third pitch. It was a bouncing grounder that got past the shortstop. I ran like crazy and was safe on first. A lot of the kids on my team cheered for me. After my strikeout in the last game, I think they were amazed to see me get on base. Gordie Corrigan was up next and hit one way out into right field. I took off and was halfway to second when I stepped on my shoelace. I went down like a ton of bricks.

Gordie rounded first and headed toward me. "Get up and run, you idiot!"

The second baseman tagged me out, then threw to first where Gordie was trying to get back on base. As we walked off the field, Gordie said, "That should have been a triple. Instead you made two outs. I don't know why they let you play with normal kids, anyway. Don't they have a special school for cripples?"

It had hurt way back when Leon had said that

everybody stares at a cripple, but he was just being honest. Gordie was using the word as a weapon.

Leon didn't try to make me feel better this time. "You don't have to play baseball, you know. You could get an excuse from your doctor."

"My doctor wants me to play."

"Well, the other guys aren't so keen on it. Gordie is going around telling everybody that any team you play on is going to lose."

"Gordie is a jerk."

"I know he is, but he has a big mouth and he has it in for you. That's all I'm saying."

That night after supper I shut myself in my room and vowed that I wouldn't come out again until I could tie my shoelaces. At first I thought I would be up all night. I tried everything I could think of and nothing worked. Finally, I discovered that if I held one end of the lace down with my stump, I could wrap the other lace around it to make a single knot. Then I made a loop and held it with my stump as I brought the other lace over it, and tucked it down through the space by the knot. It took a while to get the knot tight and still make the equal-sized loops. I kept at it until I could do it fast. My shoelace problems were over.

Band was turning out to be pretty boring. We only had it on Monday, Wednesday, and Friday. Most of the kids had never played an instrument before, so Mr. Margolus had to take a lot of time with each section while the rest of us just sat around. It was prime daydreaming time, so I didn't mind all that much.

At the beginning of Friday's band period Mr. Margolus said, "I still have the mellophone here, people. Anybody want to give it a try?" Nobody did. I was surprised, because the mellophone was a beautiful instrument. It was shiny brass, with a big bell and tubing that wrapped around in a circle like a French horn.

Mr. Margolus gave up and went over to the trumpet section. Some of the guys on trumpet couldn't even get out a sound at first. "Blow like this with your lips," he said, making a noise like a raspberry. The trumpeters all tried it and laughed. "Again. Let the air vibrate through those lips." This time a few kids got the hang of it. Gary Schroeder was spraying spit all over the place. Finally, Mr. Margolus had them blow into the trumpets. It sounded like a flock of geese being chased by dogs. Mr. Margolus had to be the most patient teacher in the school, because he didn't run screaming from the room. He kept working with the trumpet section until they were playing something that almost sounded like notes.

"Now, trombones, sousaphone, and tuba, you need to do the same thing with your lips. Try it first without your instruments." They did and we all laughed.

"Now, blow the same way into your mouthpiece." There were a few goose noises from the trombones and sousaphone. Ronnie Cressman wasn't making any sound at all with the tuba, but his face was getting red from trying. Then all of a sudden there was a blast that sounded like a farting elephant. "Excellent, Cressman," Mr. Margolus yelled. "It's not easy to get a note from a tuba. Let's hear it again." Ronnie let loose with another one, and half the band was on the floor laughing.

Next, Mr. Margolus worked with the girls on the clarinets. They were as bad as the trumpets, only they sounded like cats in heat. I had no idea playing an instrument could be so hard. It was amazing that music existed at all.

He never got to our section the first day, but how hard could it be to hit a drum? While I was day-dreaming in band, I got thinking about Jamboree. The hardest part about fire building was the flint and steel. I read in my scout handbook that each person on the team would have to prove he could do it. I tried, but I couldn't hold the flint tight enough with my stump. If I asked them to bend the rules, Gordie would never let me hear the end of it. I decided if I had learned to tie my laces, I could do the knots for Jamboree.

When I got home, I cut off a hunk of rope from Mom's extra clothesline in the garage and started practicing. When I sat down and put the rope in my lap, I could follow the diagrams in the handbook. The hard part was pulling the knot tight. I had to hold down one end with my stump while I pulled the other end with my hand. It took a while to get the hang of it, but by the end of the week I could tie all five of the required knots.

When Leon came over Friday night, I told him my plan.

"How can you compete in knot tying? You can't even tie your shoelaces."

"Oh, yeah? Watch this." I undid my shoelace and tied it. "Ta dah!"

"That's pretty good, Norm. No more tripping over your laces in gym, huh?"

"You think that's good? Get a load of this." I did all five scout knots, one after the other.

I could tell Leon was impressed, but he didn't say anything until I finished.

"I didn't think you'd be able to do that with one hand. That's really great."

"I know, but do you think it's good enough to be on the team?"

"Yeah, well, except for one thing."

"What?"

"Maybe it won't matter. Besides, you've worked really hard."

"What's wrong? Spit it out."

"You can't tie knots sitting down for the contest at Jamboree, Norm."

Leon was right. I'd been concentrating so hard on learning the knots, I hadn't even thought about the fact that they wouldn't let me tie them on my lap. "So I'll learn to tie them standing up. I have until Monday night to practice."

"Why don't we just stick with fire building?" Leon asked.

"You know Gordie's going to be the team captain, Leon." I didn't even tell him what I'd read in the handbook. Just thinking about working under Gordie was enough to convince him.

"Okay, you're right. Monday night we'll tell Mr. Palmer we want to switch."

That weekend I alternated between practicing baseball and drilling myself on knot tying. I discovered if I held the rope against my chest, it was almost like tying knots on my lap. By Monday night, I was convinced I could make the team.

Mr. Palmer was surprised that Leon and I wanted to switch. "You sure you want to do this, Norm? I can only have a team of four. Six of you are going for it." I think he wanted to say something about me having one hand, but he didn't.

"That's okay," I said. "I can do it."

"You and Leon did a nice job with the fire building."

Gordie snorted and waved the end of his neckerchief. Leon gave him a dirty look.

"We both really want to do knots, sir," I said.

He sighed. "All right. I'm judging on speed and accuracy. Who's first?"

I stepped forward. "I'll go."

Mr. Palmer pulled out his stopwatch. "Square knot first. Ready, set, go."

I went as fast as I could without dropping the rope. Right over left, left over right, and pull tight. "Done," I said.

Mr. Palmer looked surprised as he checked my knot. "That's good, Norm. Really good. You must have practiced hard for this. Next is the bowline."

I went through the steps in my head as I worked. Make a loop, bring the end up through the loop, around the standing part, and back down through the loop. "Done."

"Check," Mr. Palmer said. He was smiling now. "Sheepshank next."

This one was hard for me, but I had practiced it

more than the other knots. I tied it fine, but I pulled it so tight I had trouble untying it to do the next knot, so I lost a lot of time. The last two were the surgeon's knot and the stopper knot. I fumbled a little, but I was careful to leave them loose enough to untie.

"Two minutes, seven seconds." Mr. Palmer wrote down my score. "Nice job. That's a good time, and no deductions for sloppiness. Who's next?"

Leon went second. He wasn't doing as well as usual. He even dropped the rope during the sheepshank and had to start it over. I thought I might have a chance to beat him, but his final time was faster by twenty-three seconds. Ronnie was after Leon. It was like watching a movie in slow motion, which was weird, because he was good with knots. He got a lot of practice lassoing pigs on the farm. He beat my time by only thirteen seconds.

That's when I started to catch on. "Are you guys slowing down because you feel sorry for me and don't want to beat me?"

"Naw, Norm," Leon said. "We're just having a bad night."

"You all had better shape up or this team isn't going to beat anybody," Mr. Palmer said. "We always win this event at Jamboree, so I want to take the four best knot tiers for my team. Norm wouldn't want it any other way, would you, Norm?"

"No, sir. May the best four win." I said that because I was sure my time would hold up against a couple of the last three, especially Carl Oberndorfer. Maybe he was just nervous because he was new and didn't know anybody, but he was the clumsiest knot tier I'd ever seen. And Gary Schroeder could never remember anything, so I figured he'd mess up a knot or two.

Gary went last. When he finished, we all knew who the four best knot tiers were. Leon was one of them. So were Ronnie and goofy Gary. Clumsy Carl didn't make the team.

Neither did I.

Chapter 12

*I*t wasn't until our third band rehearsal, on Wednesday, that we finally got a song to play. Turns out it wasn't as exciting as I'd hoped it would be. Think "Twinkle, Twinkle, Little Star" performed by a bunch of honking geese, howling cats, and a farting elephant. There was a part for the bass drum, only it wasn't on the beat, the way you would tap your foot. It was somewhere between the beats, and I never could hit it right.

"On the upbeat, Schmidt," Mr. Margolus yelled. "AND one AND two AND three AND four AND twin-KLE twin-KLE li-TLE sta-AR. Feel it in your bones, Schmidt. Feel it in your bones. BOOM one BOOM two BOOM three BOOM four BOOM."

I didn't feel it in my bones. I didn't feel it anywhere but in my head, which was aching from all the noise. By Friday, I knew I didn't want to play the bass drum. The other kids were working on scales and learning melody and harmony. All I was doing was boom, boom, boom. Sure I was in the band, but everybody knew the poor one-handed kid couldn't do anything except bang a drum like a baby hitting pots from his mother's kitchen cupboard with a wooden spoon.

We had moved on to "Way Down upon the Swanee River." This time I played on the beat but only once in a while. Bass drum is not a good instrument for a daydreamer. We started and stopped so much, I only had one boom every six or seven minutes. The rest of the time I had to count beats until it was time to come in. Mr. Margolus was constantly yelling at me. "Schmidt! Where's the boom? I want to hear that boom." Carl Oberndorfer tried to give me cues, but he was busy with his snare-drum part, which was pretty complicated. After him being so clumsy with the knots in scouts, I was surprised that he could play the drums so well.

I kept eyeing that mellophone that nobody wanted to play. It looked like a piece of brass sculpture. It had keys like the trumpet that you played with your right hand. After band period was over, Mr. Margolus left the room with the kids. When everybody was gone, I picked up the mellophone. It was heavy, but I could balance the weight of it on my stump. I blew in the mouthpiece and made a pretty good sound. I pressed on a key and got another note. I experimented with all the keys, then picked out the melody to "Twinkle, Twinkle, Little Star." I even knew how to make the notes between the keys, because I had been listening to Mr. Margolus teach the trumpets the scale.

Suddenly, I heard clapping. Mr. Margolus came into the band room. "So, Schmidt, I finally have my mellophone player?"

"Maybe, sir," I said.

"Try holding it like this." He moved my left arm so my stump was inside the bell of the horn.

"Won't that block out the sound like muting the trumpet?"

"No. That's the way you're supposed to hold it."

I tried playing a few notes. "Yeah, that's much easier."

Then Mr. Margolus showed me how to play the scale, so I'd know the notes for sure instead of guessing. "You're picking this up very quickly, Schmidt. Your talent was being wasted on the bass drum."

"This is more fun," I said.

"I'm glad you feel that way. Listen, since you're getting a late start with the mellophone, would you like to sign it out for the weekend to practice?"

"Sure, that would be great."

Mr. Margolus wrote down my name and the date in his notebook. "Hurry back to your classroom now. We don't want you to miss your bus."

Miss Bean looked up when I ran into her room. Most of the class had gone. "I wondered where you were, Norman. What's in the case?"

"A mellophone," I said. "Mr. Margolus is letting me have it over the weekend." I opened my desk and took the three books I needed for homework.

"That's quite a load to carry with your instrument, Norman. You may use this for your books if you'd like." Miss Bean held out a leather bag.

"A purse?"

Miss Bean laughed. "It's not a purse. It's a book bag."

"No offense, Miss Bean, but it sure looks like a purse to me."

"All right. I just thought it might make things easier."

Having no homework would make things easier, but Miss Bean and I had already been through that. I held the books with my stump and picked up the mellophone. I wouldn't be caught dead carrying a purse. And I didn't care what Miss Bean said. That's exactly what that bag was.

Ronnie took the seat next to me on the bus. "Hey, Norm, whatcha got?"

"The mellophone."

"No kidding? That's neat. So how come you get to take it home?"

"Mr. Margolus thought I could use some practice time to catch up."

Ronnie nodded. He was quiet for a minute, then he said, "You must have worked hard on the knots for scouts. You should've made the team."

"It was fair and square. My time wasn't good enough."

"Still, you should've made it."

"You did your part by slowing down. Leon's kind of flaky, so it didn't surprise me that he dropped the rope, but when you looked like you were swimming in mashed potatoes, I knew something was going on."

Ronnie ducked his head and grinned. "It was just me and Leon that cooked up the plan. Nobody else was in on it."

"Thanks for trying to help, Ronnie, but I have to do things for myself."

"Yeah, that's what my cousin Arnie always says."

Ronnie made that chopping motion on his arm, to remind me that Arnie was the cousin who'd lost his arm—as if I could ever forget. "Arnie's doing real good for himself now. He got a job in the Carmel Savings and Loan."

I wondered what it would be like to work in a bank. Sounded boring, but at least Arnie wasn't selling pencils. That was a good thing to know.

When I got off the bus at home, Mom came out of the store. "What's this?" she asked, patting the instrument case.

"A mellophone," I said. "I'm the only mellophone player in the whole band."

Mom smiled. "Well, what do you know? I don't think I ever met a mellophone player before."

"I'm supposed to practice over the weekend," I said.

"That's fine, but I'm afraid the practice will have to wait until later, Norm. Somebody brought in a huge load of return bottles today. We need you to sort them out because we're tripping over them. So change out of your school clothes and come right down to the store."

I had been planning to stay upstairs and listen to a baseball game. It was the playoffs, and I got some good tips on how to improve my game from the guys calling the plays. Dad had an old radio in the back room of the store that I could take outside where the bottle-sorting crates were. I used the extension cord to reach the plug in the back room, then moved Dad's wire antenna around until the New York station came in clear.

I set to work sorting the bottles into the right

wooden crates to send back to the bottling plants. There were crates for Coca-Cola, Canada Dry, Royal Crown, Pepsi, and Nehi for the sodas, and Pabst Blue Ribbon, Rheingold, Schlitz, and Ballantine for the beers. The flies and yellow jackets were already buzzing around, trying to get to the liquid left in the bottoms of the bottles.

Listening to the radio made the time go faster. It was the bottom of the fifth, so I had already missed a lot of the game. Then the announcer said something that caught my attention.

"Number nine, Ted Williams, is coming up to the plate. He has a .342 batting average so far this year. It's interesting that he bats left-handed even though he throws with his right."

The other announcer said, "How much of that record do you think is due to his batting left-handed, Joe?"

"What does that have to do with it?"

"Well, the left-handed batting position is on the right side of the batter's box. It gives him a shorter distance to run to first base."

"I could see how that might make a difference for a weaker hitter, Mel, but Williams doesn't need that edge."

I could hear the crack of the bat and the crowd cheering.

"Williams hits a high chopper to third. It's fielded by Snuffy Stirnweiss with a long throw to Nick Etten at first."

"Holy cow! Williams beats it out at first. You might have a point about that left-hand edge, Joe."

Maybe Ted Williams didn't need an edge, but I sure could use one. I'd switch to batting left-handed. I went over to my batting spot, picked up my bat, and swung at the hanging ball. It felt like a much stronger swing because I was pulling my right arm all the way across my body. I tried it again and it was even better.

This was fantastic! Not only did I have a stronger swing this way, but I had that one-step head start from being on the right side of the batter's box. Cutting just one second off my time could make the difference between being safe or out at first. That's when I decided to become the world's first left-handed batter without a left hand.

Chapter 13

Before we knew it, it was the end of September—Jamboree weekend. Our patrol left right after school so we could get to Taconic State Park early enough to set up the tents before dark. Our troop had two four-man tents with cots, but the older guys always got those. The kids in our group slept on the ground in two-man tents. It was pretty warm for September, so sleeping on the ground was no problem. Leon and I were the first two to get our tent set up.

Mr. Palmer came over to see if we had the stakes pounded in right. "Nice job, boys. Don't forget to dig a trench around your tent, though."

"It's not supposed to rain all weekend, Mr. Palmer," Leon said. "Mr. Weatheright on the radio said so."

"That man should be named Mr. Weatherwrong, because he is wrong more than half the time. If you don't want to be sleeping in a puddle, you'd better start digging." Mr. Palmer handed Leon the shovel. "Take this over to the next tent when you're finished digging. Then come help with dinner."

Leon and I took turns digging our trench, then

passed on the shovel to the guys in the next tent and headed over to our campfire.

Gordie's team was in charge of building the fire for dinner. As usual, he was bossing everybody around. He was just about to light the fire with his Zippo when Ken, an older kid who was our patrol leader, took the lighter from him and handed him the flint and steel kit. "You need to practice for tomorrow."

Gordie pawned the job off on another kid, then kept telling him that he wasn't doing it right.

"We'll be eating our hot dogs raw with Gordie in charge," I said. "Let's go look around and see which other troops are here."

Cars were still arriving for the Jamboree. A station wagon pulled into the next campsite, and four kids our age got out. I recognized a couple of them from last year's camping trips and Jamborees. They came from a troop in Mahopac. Leon and I helped them unload their gear. When I handed one of the kids a rucksack, he noticed my missing hand. His eyes almost bugged out of his head. "Holy cow! What happened to you?"

"I had an accident."

"A car accident?"

"His father owns a meat market," Leon said. "Norm lost his hand in the meat grinder."

By now the other three kids had gathered around. "No kidding?" the tall one said. "That's awful. Does it hurt?"

I shrugged. "Not so much anymore. I'm used to it by now."

"Yeah," Leon said. "He's right-handed, so he didn't use that one much anyway."

Just then we heard an owl hoot. "That's our troop leader calling us back," I said, giving Leon a shove toward our campsite. "We'll see you later."

When we got out of earshot, I said, "For Pete's sake, Leon, do you have to go around telling everybody I lost my hand in a meat grinder?"

"What do you want me to say? That you set it down someplace and couldn't remember where you put it?"

"You don't have to say anything. I can do my own talking. And what was that stupid comment about me not using my left hand anyway?"

"I said you didn't use it as much as your right hand. That's true, isn't it?"

"I don't care. I just don't want to talk about it."

"Well, lots of luck. These kids are going to ask about it, Norm. None of them have seen you since the accident."

I hadn't thought about that. Most of my friends from home were getting used to me having only one hand, but to strangers I was still a freak. Here I was feeling like things were getting back to normal, but every time I met somebody I'd have to deal with the whole thing all over again.

"I wondered what happened to you boys." We were back at our campsite and Mr. Palmer was coming toward us. "Take a couple of those green sticks and get your hot dogs ready."

I had never given a second thought about how to put a hot dog on a stick before, but trying to do it with one hand was tough. Sure, I could hold the stick under my left arm and get started poking it though the end of the hot dog. But when I watched Leon, he was steering the stick through the hot dog with his left hand so it stayed in the center from end to end. My stick got off track and came through the skin a couple of inches from the beginning.

"You want me to fix that, Norm?" Leon asked.

"No, it's fine. It's not going anywhere."

There was only one side of the fire that was really burning well, and the cooks had hung the pot of canned beans over that, so we all had to shove our hot dogs together in one little spot to cook them. Mine was cooking just on one end. Then somebody's stick knocked against mine and my hot dog dropped into the fire.

"Oops! Tough luck, Norm," Gordie said, grinning.

"Not a problem," I said. "I like mine grilled in the coals."

Actually, my hot dog wasn't bad, once I wiped the ashes off it. It was better than the beans, which were half cold and half burned.

"If Gordie's fire for the competition is like this one, we aren't going to be putting any blue ribbons on our flagpole for fire building," Leon mumbled.

We washed down our hot dogs and beans with Kool-Aid. Even though the food wasn't like Mom's home cooking, everything always tasted good when you ate it outdoors. After we cleaned up our mess kits and put out our fire, we headed to the main campfire for the opening ceremony.

Mr. Carnahan, the head of the Boy Scout Council, took roll call. There were troops from five other towns besides Lake Carmel—Mahopac, Brewster, Patterson, Bedford Hills, and Golden's Bridge. Each troop sat together around the campfire. The older guys from our troop had dragged some big logs over near the fire for us to sit on. I always liked this part of camping out, just when everybody gets settled in. It was dark, so our fronts were hot from the fire, but we could feel the cold on our backs.

Mr. Carnahan had us sing a few camp songs first. We started out with "B-I-N-G-O," then "You Can't Get to Heaven." The kids from Mahopac wanted to sing "99 Bottles of Beer on the Wall" after that.

"No time tonight, boys. We'll save that for the closing campfire tomorrow night. We have some business to take care of. First, most of you probably already know you get your water from the faucet over by the entry road. Gather your firewood in the woods behind cabin number three. Troops 41, 73, and 22 use latrine number one, and the rest of you use latrine number two."

Leon started to raise his hand.

"What are you doing?" I whispered.

"I'm going to ask Mr. Carnahan if we can use latrine number one for number two."

I punched him in the arm and he folded up laughing.

"Did we have a question from troop number 22?" Mr. Carnahan asked.

"Sorry, sir, just stretching," Leon said.

Mr. Palmer came over and sat next to Leon, ready to squelch any trouble before it started. Leon didn't mean anything by it. He was just being Leon.

As Mr. Carnahan went on to list the competitions the next day, I looked around. All the faces reflected the orange light from the fire, and the woods behind were a deep purple. I studied the way the firelight made deep shadows around everybody's eyes, memorizing it, so if I ever got a good set of paints—like oil paints—I'd know how to paint a scene just like this. I used to ask for paints every year for Christmas, but I never got them. Dad didn't think art was very practical. I'd just have to earn the money to buy them myself.

I came out of my painting daydream to hear Mr. Carnahan talk about the first-aid competition. "I hope you all got the instructions we sent out about the new rules for this Jamboree. You're to have your first-aid team divided into two groups as usual: the victims and the persons giving aid. The difference this time is that you won't be treating victims from your own team. You'll be working on scouts from competing teams. So let's come up with some tough situations for the other team to handle, but keep it within reason. Fractures, wounds, and burns are fine, but nothing disastrous like an amputation."

"Good thing you're not on first aid, Norm," Leon whispered. "You'd be disqualified right off the bat."

Mr. Palmer glanced over at Leon but looked too embarrassed to say anything.

It was funny, but I felt more comfortable with Leon's remark than I did with Mr. Palmer's embarrassment.

Leon was always giving me grief about something. It was only natural that he'd tease me about the hand. I think it was his way of saying that, for him, I was the same person I always was.

After a few more announcements, we sang "Taps" and the meeting broke up. It was late by the time we got back to our own campsite. Without a campfire going there was nothing to do, so we all went to our own tents.

"Wanna tell ghost stories?" Leon asked, when we got settled into our sleeping bags.

"That's no fun with just two guys."

"Well, then we could sneak out and bug people. How about we go scare Gordie?"

"He's already after us all the time. You want to give him an excuse to get us in trouble?"

"He doesn't have to know it's us."

"You go scare Gordie. Leave me out of it."

Leon didn't say anything else, and I thought he had fallen asleep. But he wasn't sleeping. He was scheming. It's a wonder I didn't hear his brain cells grinding together. All of a sudden he was shining his flashlight in my eyes. "Norm! Do you know what's going to be so neat?"

"No, what?"

"When you get your hook."

"You woke me up to tell me that?"

Leon tugged at my sleeping bag. "No, really, you gotta hear this. Sit up."

"My ears work perfectly well lying down."

"All right. Listen. You know that story one of the older kids told last year, about the one-armed guy who snuck around Lover's Lane and killed couples who were making out?"

"Yeah. So?"

"So this one couple think they hear somebody outside their car and it creeps them out, on account of they heard about the one-armed guy in the news. So the kid starts the car and drives out of there fast, and when they get home, they find a hook caught in their door handle?"

"Yeah, yeah, I know the story. Everybody knows that story. Somebody tells it every year."

"That's what makes this so good." Leon pounded on his sleeping bag. "Oh, man, this is going to be perfect. Next year we'll tell the story at the campfire, just before everybody goes to bed. Then we'll sneak around Gordie's tent. You can scratch on the tent with your hook. Then we'll leave it so they find the hook in the morning and think the one-armed guy was sneaking around their tent."

"Or they'll think the one-handed kid in their scout troop was sneaking around their tent and they'll come over and clobber him with his own hook. That is so lame, Leon."

"You have no sense of adventure," Leon said.

"You have no sense, period," I said. "Go to sleep."

The next morning, after breakfast, Mr. Palmer had me signed up for the orienteering team, but Bill Gordon from the first-aid team called me over. "Hey, Norm, we need you to do us a favor."

"You heard what Mr. Carnahan said. No amputations. So if you're planning on putting catsup on the end of my stump and having me pretend I just got my hand cut off, you can forget it."

"Heck, no," Bill said. "That sounds like something Leon would think up."

"Yeah. I guess I've been hanging around him too long. What did you want me for anyway?"

"Charlie Ackerman brought some great stuff for fake wounds, but none of us can make it look real. You could do it, though. You're a good artist."

Charlie's father was the town undertaker. Charlie had brought a big hunk of his father's mortician's wax and some makeup. "This stuff isn't used, is it?" I asked.

"Naw, it's from a new batch," Charlie said. "I brought blood, too." He swirled some thick red liquid around in a bottle.

"This isn't from . . ."

Charlie grinned. "Real bodies? Are you kidding? Dad doesn't even let me near where he does his . . . you know. I made this stuff from corn syrup and red food coloring."

I took the bottle from him. It looked pretty realistic. "We should put this on the pancakes tomorrow morning—gross everybody out."

Bill held out his arm. "C'mon, Norm. Give me a cool-looking wound. Something really gruesome."

I started fooling around with the wax, warming it up in my hand so I could mold it into a scar. Then I had a great idea. I built up a long lump of wax on the inside of Bill's wrist, smoothing off the edges so it blended into his skin. I molded a tendon and smoothed that out, too. "Give me your scout knife, Bill."

"What for? I want a fake wound, not a real one."

"Very funny." I opened the knife and gently sliced through the wax on Bill's arm.

Bill tried to pull away. "You're not going to cut me, are you?"

"Not if you hold still, I'm not."

When I got the knife blade deep enough into the wax, it looked like Bill had plunged it into his arm. "Hold this in place," I said. I built up the edges of the fake flesh to hold the knife steady. Then I took the makeup and matched the color of Bill's skin and painted the inside of the wound dark red, like you could see the muscle. The final touch was a squirt of blood. It looked so real, Bill almost threw up.

Carl Oberndorfer took one look and ran out of the campsite. Mr. Palmer had assigned him to first aid when he didn't make the knot-tying team. Now he probably wouldn't get to compete in anything, but it wasn't my fault that he had a weak stomach.

I had another great idea. "Does anybody have a fishhook?"

"I do," Charlie said. "I brought my fishing pole."

"Go get it."

When he came back with the pole, I had Charlie sit down and lean his head back. Then I put a glob of wax over the end of the hook, and pressed the whole thing into his neck, just below his ear. I used a toothpick to enlarge the hole around the fishhook, pulling the wax down so it looked like the hook was dragging it. I left the line and pole attached for realism. Then I added just a small amount of blood around the hook.

Everybody crowded around to admire my handi-work.

"I want to see what I look like," Charlie said. "Any-body have a mirror?"

"Sorry, I left my mirror home with my lipstick," Bill said. "You think this is a *Girl* Scout troop, Ackerman?"

"Wait," Charlie said. "My mess kit is brand-new. I bet I can see my reflection in the plate." He ran over to his tent and came back with the metal plate. He looked so funny carrying the pole with the hook stuck in his neck, we all laughed.

"Now give me a fracture, Norm—a compound one." It was Carl. He was holding the bone from a chicken drumstick.

"Where did you get that?" I asked.

"The troop from Mahopac had fried chicken last night. I got it out of their garbage."

The bone was too small to be from a person's leg, so I decided to give Carl a fractured wrist. Carl broke the bone over a pointed rock to give it splintered ends. Then I built up the wound with wax and imbedded the bone so it looked like it was jutting out from Carl's arm. I blended the wax into his skin and molded a piece to look like a bunched-up muscle that had been torn away from the bone. Then I added details with the makeup, using different shades of red for the muscle. I was getting really good at this.

Carl must have been thinking the same thing. "Do you know how to make this stuff look realistic because you remember what your arm looked like when you had your accident, Norm?"

"Nah. I know how muscles look from watching my father cut up a side of beef. I couldn't see anything when I had my accident. My hand was way down in the meat grinder."

"Was there a lot of blood?" Charlie asked.

"No. The doctor said the meat grinder had me clamped down like a tourniquet. I hardly bled at all."

It seemed perfectly natural to be talking with the guys about the day I lost my hand. I also realized that as I did each guy's makeup, I had been steadying his arm or neck with my stump, and nobody was creeped out about that, either. I think it was the first time I had touched another person with my stump, except maybe for hugging Mom.

I put the final touches on Carl's fracture, squirting some blood into the wound and even a little in the center of the splintered bone to look like marrow.

Just then I saw Gordie heading toward us. Maybe I was feeling like hot stuff over doing such a great job on the wounds, because I did something that was more like Leon than me. "Pretend you really broke your arm," I whispered to Carl.

Carl grabbed his arm, making sure the broken bone showed. "Somebody help me!" he moaned.

Gordie came running over. "What are you blubbering about, you little sissy?" Then his eyes landed on the chicken bone. "Holy cow, Carl, what did you do to yourself?"

"I tripped," Carl said, then dissolved into some pretty realistic-sounding sobs.

"You'd better go get Mr. Palmer," I said. "We'll stay here and keep Carl calm."

As Gordie ran off, Carl really got into the act, rocking back and forth holding his arm.

"You ought to get an Oscar for this performance," I said, and Carl broke up laughing.

"Watch it. Here they come," Charlie whispered, and Carl went back into his act.

Mr. Palmer's face turned white when he saw Carl's arm. He knelt down. "Carl, what happened?"

Before we could say anything, Gordie interrupted. "He tripped, Mr. Palmer. I saw the whole thing. Norm was trying to get Carl up on his feet, but I remembered the rule—'Splint him where he lies'—so I wouldn't let anybody move him. Especially with his bone sticking out like that. Norm should have known better. That's a compound fracture. Very dangerous. I told everybody to stay right where they were until I came back with you."

"Pipe down, Gordie," Mr. Palmer said.

Carl couldn't help it. He started laughing. Then he tried to cover it up with some more moans.

Mr. Palmer looked closely at the wound. Then he sat back and noticed the fishhook sticking out of Charlie's neck and the knife plunged into Bill's arm. "What the . . . these are all fake wounds? Who did this?"

"They're fake?" Gordie said, his face turning red.

"You boys really had me going," Mr. Palmer said, standing up. "This is remarkable work. Who's the artist?"

"Norm did them all," Charlie said.

"I know I was supposed to do orienteering, sir. I got sidetracked."

Mr. Palmer patted me on the back. "Don't worry

about it, Norm. I wouldn't be a bit surprised if you just won the first-aid event for us."

Gordie gave a disgusted grunt and walked away. I finished the team with an impressive second-degree burn for Freddie Grabb, complete with blisters made out of sliced white grapes and some extra grape skins thrown in for broken blisters. Carl fished around the campfire and came up with old charred marshmallow skins, which I stuck on to make a third-degree burn. Everybody agreed it was truly disgusting.

We easily won the first-aid competition. We were up against the strongest team. They were so shook-up by the realistic wounds, they panicked and couldn't think of what the treatment should be, especially when our guys acted like they were in agony. When we were announced as the winners, Mr. Palmer introduced me to the whole group as the team artist. Gordie was really sore, but he didn't give me any more grief. His fire-building team had come in last.

That night for the campfire, we used the makeup to do a skit about an accident-prone scout troop. I played the part of Mr. Palmer, running around getting hysterical as each scout came in with a gruesome injury. We were the hit of the closing-night campfire, and Mr. Palmer laughed harder than anybody.

Chapter 14

*H*alloween came around before we knew it. The younger kids had a costume parade in the gym. Some of the fifth- and sixth-graders wore costumes, mostly simple stuff from old clothes, like gypsies or hobos.

I was planning to practice baseball when I got home from school, but Dad heard the school bus and called to me from the store. "The truck from Acme Rendering is due in less than an hour, Norm. Run upstairs and change into your old clothes so you can get the fat ready for them."

Next to emptying the garbage, this was my least favorite job. Ever since the beginning of the war, people were supposed to pour the fat drippings from cooking meat into tin cans and take them to their butcher. Once a week the truck came from the rendering plant to pick up the cans. We got paid four cents a pound for what we collected. Somehow the stuff went into making things like shampoo, linoleum, and nylon stockings. When you drove by Acme Rendering, the smell would make you gag even with all the car windows closed.

I pulled on my work dungarees and an old T-shirt and ran down the stairs. I almost knocked Leon over when I opened the outside door.

"Hey, watch it, Norm. What's your rush?"

"I have to get the fat loaded up. I could use some help."

"I gotta tell you about my plan." He waved a piece of paper in my face.

"If I don't have the fat ready, the guy won't wait around. It'll stink to high heaven if it has to be here another full week, and I'll be grounded for sure."

"Okay, okay! I'll tell you about it while we work." He shoved the paper back in his pocket and followed me through the store.

Mom looked up from the cash register. "Norman, you have work to do."

"He told me, Mrs. Schmidt," Leon said. "I'm going to help him."

Mom shook her head. She knew how much work I'd get out of Leon.

I pulled out an empty cardboard carton. "Start loading them into here."

Leon picked up a greasy can and made a face. "Why are you still doing this? I thought you could stop collecting fat when the war was over."

Dad came out of the cold room carrying a ham. "This country used to get a lot of the fat we needed from overseas, Leon, but that stopped with the war and hasn't started again. The Europeans can't afford to eat as much meat as before."

"Very interesting, Mr. Schmidt. I didn't know that."

Leon pretended to help me until Dad was back at the meat counter. "Here's my map. We go to all the houses between West Lakeshore Drive and Route 52. We ring the doorbell, yell 'trick or treat,' hold out our bags for candy, and yell 'thank you' while running to the next house. We can hit one every minute. That's a hundred and twenty houses between six and eight o'clock. Can you imagine the haul we'll get?"

"Why do you want so much? It'll get stale before you can eat it all."

"More people gave out candy before we had sugar rationing," Leon said. "So we increase our odds of getting candy by going to more houses."

He was right. Some people gave apples, nuts, or popcorn. We didn't have as much candy in the store because the candy companies had rationing, too.

Leon stabbed his finger on his map. "See where I have the arrows? That's where we run through back yards to get from one street to the next instead of going all the way to the corners. What do you think?"

"I think you're not helping me with these cans. That's what I think."

I pulled out a second carton and began loading it up. "I also think you've forgotten what slows us down the most."

"What's that?"

"My sister."

"Aw, Norm. Do we have to take Ellie with us? She always has to go inside to show off her stupid fairy costume. Besides, it's going to be cold tonight, so she'll have to take off her coat and twirl around to show those tinsel wings. That's going to take a good five minutes per house. That means we'll only be able to hit . . ." He scribbled something on the back of his map and then smacked himself on the forehead. "Only twelve houses an hour, Norm. Only twenty-four houses total because we have to be in by eight. Can't your mom take Ellie out?"

"Mom has to work in the store. And I can't even go out until seven because I have to hand out candy until the store closes."

Leon slumped down on a case of canned corn. "Twelve lousy houses! I don't believe this. I spent all that time walking around the neighborhood, making the map, and timing everything. It was such a great plan."

"Nothing has changed from last year, Leon."

"I know," Leon moaned. "I just got so hepped up about my map, I forgot." He was quiet for about two seconds, then jumped up. "Hey, I just got another idea, though. How about you use this for your costume?" He picked up a meat hook from the back table. "You could tape this to your arm and go as a pirate."

"Put that down. Dad would have a fit if I took it. I'm going to be a hobo."

"Yeah, me too. But next year when you have your real hook, you'll have to be a pirate for sure."

"Next year we'll be in seventh grade. We'll be too old for trick-or-treating."

"I'll never be too old to go out and have people give me candy. You're nuts, Norm."

I finished loading the second carton and shoved it toward him with my foot. "You can carry that one." I lifted my box and lugged it out the back door. Leon followed me. We piled the boxes next to the big steel barrels Dad had already put out there. The rendering plant took all of our leftover bones and the animal hides from slaughtering pigs. I didn't even want to know what they made out of those.

Leon was staring at the restaurant next door. Marion Schneider had just come out the back door with a carton of grease cans for the rendering truck. "Hey, Marion," Leon yelled. "Wait a minute."

"We can't stay out here talking," I said. "We have to get the rest of the fat."

"Go ahead. I'll be right back." He trotted across the parking lot to Marion.

I couldn't believe it. Was he going soft in the head about girls now? And Marion was in eighth grade. She wouldn't give a sixth-grade boy a tumble.

I was just taking out the last carton when Leon came back. "Nice timing," I said. "I barely finished in time for the truck."

Leon looked around. "I don't see any truck."

"I don't see it, either. I smell it, though."

Leon wrinkled his nose. "Oh, man, so do I. Let's get inside." We held our noses and ran for the door as the big flatbed truck pulled in. Leon headed straight for my mother, who was refilling the chewing-gum display. "Mrs. Schmidt, I was just talking with Marion Schneider from next door at the Happy Valley."

"That's nice, Leon. How is Marion?"

"She's fine, Mrs. Schmidt. She told me that she's taking her little sister out trick-or-treating tonight, and she wondered if Ellie would like to go with them."

Ellie stuck her head around the magazine rack. "Oh, could I, Mommy? When I go with Norm and Leon, they want to rush away before I get a chance to go inside and be the Blue Fairy."

Mom looked at me. "You do take the time to thank people for the candy, don't you, Norman?"

"We sure do, Mrs. Schmidt," Leon said. "That's definitely part of our plan."

"If you want to go with Marion, that's fine, Ellie," Mom said. "Just make sure you're back by eight."

I grinned at Leon, but I could tell he wasn't finished. He was clearing his throat. "And I was wondering if you could do us a little favor, Mrs. Schmidt."

"What would that little favor be, Leon?"

"Would you mind handing out the candy here in the store, so Norm and I could start out at six instead of seven?"

I couldn't believe he had asked that. Dad came around from behind the meat counter. "You want me giving away candy in my store, Leon? Bad enough I get kids in here who sneak candy into their pockets, but you think I should hand it to the little hoodlums to save them the trouble of stealing? And would that keep them from soaping my store window? Not a chance."

I didn't know why Dad always got so mad about the soaped window. I was the one who had to clean it off after Halloween. I grabbed Leon's arm and pulled him out of the store. "Nice play, Shakespeare. You're lucky Dad didn't go into the speech about how he doesn't like his kids going out to the neighbors and begging for candy. Geez! What were you thinking?"

"Sorry, Norm. I thought it was a pretty good idea. Anyway I solved one of our problems. Without Ellie, we can still hit sixty houses."

"All right," I said. "Pick me up at seven."

I only managed to fit in about fifteen minutes of baseball practice before supper, but it was better than nothing. I figured if I tried to practice a little every day, I'd keep getting better.

After supper, Mom went back down to work in the store. Then Ellie got into her costume. Mom had given her an old, worn-down lipstick, and Ellie had put it on her lips. Well, she had tried for her lips, but she ran over the edge the way she used to miss the lines in her coloring books.

"You look like you did that in a fast-moving train," I said.

"That's not funny, Norm." I could see tears in her eyes, and I felt bad that I had made fun of her.

"All right, go wash that off and let me do it for you."

"Don't be silly. Boys don't know how to do lipstick."

She ran over to the living-room mirror. "All right. Maybe you could do it better." She went into the bathroom and came back with a clean face except for pale pink smudges all around her mouth. She handed me the lipstick. "I found blue eye shadow. Mommy never uses that, so I'm sure it's okay to take some."

"Do this." I stretched my lips the way I'd seen Mom do it when she put on lipstick for church.

Ellie copied my expression, and I drew on the lips

as if I was doing a painting. "Close your eyes." I brushed the blue stuff on her eyelids.

Ellie went to check in the mirror again. "Oh, that's beautiful, Normie. What are you going out as?"

"A hobo, I guess."

"You're always a hobo. That's a dumb costume."

"Yeah, well, I get the same candy as the Blue Fairy, so that's all that matters to me."

Ellie flounced over to the window to watch for Marion. She used to trip on the long skirt of her dress, but I noticed that it came to a little below her knees now and that the buttons on the back looked like they would pop out of the buttonholes. I had a feeling this was Ellie's last performance as the Blue Fairy.

"Here they come!" she shouted, grabbing her coat and a big paper bag. "I'll see you later, Norm."

I got my stuff together—just an old jacket of Dad's and a beat-up hat from Uncle Bill. I rubbed some charcoal on my face to look like five-o'clock shadow. It wasn't a great costume, but Leon and I were going to be standing on the front steps of each house for about fifteen seconds. People would barely be able to see us.

Whenever the doorbell rang, I had to run down the flight of stairs with the bowl of candy for trick-or-treaters. I had just climbed upstairs for about the fourteenth time when the bell rang again. Before I could start back down, Leon burst in, bounding up the stairs two at a time. "Can you get away early?"

"You know I can't leave until the store closes. What's the problem?"

Leon spread his map on the kitchen table. "We gotta change our strategy. Instead of starting at Chauncey Road, we'll have to do Mamanasco Road first."

"That's right in the middle of our route. Won't we lose time doing that?"

"Some things are more important than time, Norm."

"Not if more time means more candy. What's more important than that?"

Leon grinned. "Homemade chocolate éclairs the size of a jumbo bratwurst. An old lady on Mamanasco made them. On the way over here, I ran into some kids who were eating them. The word is out, so everybody's going to be going there first. We gotta get there before she runs out of them."

I looked at the kitchen clock. It was only six-fifteen. "You go ahead without me. No sense both of us missing out." I was sure he'd say he'd wait for me. After all, we had been trick-or-treating together since we were in kindergarten.

He didn't. "Okay, Norm. I'll see if she'll give me an extra one for you. Then I'll come back to pick you up by seven."

The doorbell rang again. Leon followed me down the stairs, then squeezed around a group of short ghosts and hobos and ran on down the street.

I didn't have high hopes for getting an éclair. Even if the lady gave Leon an extra one—which I was pretty sure she wouldn't, because most adults are on to tricks like that—there was no chance Leon would be able to carry it all the way back without gulping it down himself. He'd start out by just licking a little chocolate icing, but then something would snap inside that brain of his and he'd inhale the thing the way Knocky wolfed down his dinner. I couldn't hold that against Leon. He couldn't help it any more than Knocky could.

There was a long lull between trick-or-treaters, then the bell rang again. I grabbed the candy and went downstairs, but I didn't hear anybody yelling "trick or treat." When I opened the door, there was Carl Oberndorfer. He had bloodstained bandages all over his arms and legs, and he carried a crutch.

"Hey, Carl. That's a swell costume."

"I just ripped up my old ghost sheet and put red paint on it for blood." He held up a chicken bone. "Would you do that compound fracture for me that you did at Jamboree? I saved all the stuff."

"Sure. Come on up."

Carl followed me upstairs and laid out all the pieces of mortician's wax on the kitchen table. I started working with it, but I had to keep going downstairs to answer the door. I didn't have any of the makeup, but then I remembered Ellie's lipstick and eye shadow. I blended the red and blue in with the wax and had the bone sticking out of it.

"Gee, thanks, Norm. This looks even better than at Jamboree."

"I like doing stuff like this," I said.

"Yeah, you're going to be an artist, right?"

"Maybe. Hey, Carl, how come you're over in this neighborhood tonight? You don't live around here, do you? I never saw you on the bus."

"Yeah, I moved here with my grandmother this

fall. We live a couple of streets over from here. It's a different bus route, though. We go along by the lake."

Just then the doorbell rang again. I picked up the candy bowl, but the door opened. "Hey, Norm!" It was Leon.

He came running up the stairs. "I was too late. They were gone. All she had were lollipops."

I looked at Leon's face for telltale traces of chocolate. "I know what you're thinking. But I'm not lying. Here, I got you a lollipop."

Leon noticed Carl for the first time. "Oh, hi, Carl. Cool costume."

"Thanks. You're a hobo, right?"

Leon nodded. "So have you been out trick-or-treating yet?"

"No. I started here so Norm could do my broken bone."

The doorbell rang three more times while I was doing Carl's fracture, but Leon took over so I didn't have to go downstairs.

I pointed to Leon's bag. "You get any good stuff?"

"No, I just went to the one place then came here. I'm not trick-or-treating without you."

Carl checked out his costume in the mirror. "Cool. I'd better get going."

"Okay, Carl. Hey, who are you trick-or-treating with?"

Carl shrugged. "Nobody. I'm just going around by myself."

Leon looked at me and I nodded. "That's no fun," Leon said. "You want to go out with us?"

"Sure."

Leon pulled out his map and filled Carl in on our master plan. Then we sat on the stairs and waited for Mom to get out of the store. As soon as she showed up, we bolted like sprinters taking off from the starting block.

We got behind a few slow-moving groups of kids, so we didn't hit quite as many houses as we had planned. A lady on Chauncey Road got real upset about Carl's fracture—she thought he had fallen on their front steps and broken his arm—so we had to explain that he was okay, and we lost more time doing that. Then the lady got even more upset when she saw that my missing hand was real. Then she got all embarrassed about being upset. It took forever to get out of there, but it was worth it because she went to her kitchen and came back with a new kind of candy bar called Almond Joy for each of us. I knew from stocking our candy shelf that they were ten cents, twice as expensive as Mounds or Hershey Bars.

We were walking down Mamanasco, heading for home, when Carl stopped. "You guys want to come into my house for a minute?"

Leon squinted at the house number. "Isn't this the place where they had the éclairs?"

"Yes. My grandmother makes great éclairs. How did you hear about that?"

"Are you kidding?" Leon said. "Everybody was talking about them. She ran out, though. I was here earlier."

"I bet she saved some," Carl said. "She baked a whole bunch."

When we went into the house, Carl's grandmother said the most beautiful words I had ever heard. "Carl, you and your friends have a seat at the table and I'll bring out my secret supply of chocolate éclairs."

Carl and I each had two of them. Leon had three.

Chapter 15

Band was improving. Oh, sure, we weren't together all the time, and sometimes the trombones were flat. Well, mostly Leon, because he was always pushing the slider all the way out to poke someone instead of stopping at the right note. We were playing Christmas carols now, and since most of us knew them by heart, it was easier to make them sound like actual music. Carl turned out to be a real whiz on the snare drums. I told him that one Friday after band rehearsal.

Carl shrugged. "It's nothing. Anybody can play the snare drums."

"Not me," I said, holding up my stump.

Carl's face turned red. "I'm sorry, Norm. I didn't mean anything by it."

"Hey, it's fine. I was just making a joke." I realized I was talking to Carl the way I'd talk to Leon, expecting him to make some smart remark back to me.

"I'm not very good at jokes," Carl said.

Now it was my turn to feel bad. You never saw Carl laughing and fooling around with the other kids. He was sort of a loner, the kind of kid nobody noticed.

"How do you like playing the mellophone?" Carl asked.

"I like it fine. I take it home every weekend now. Mom plays the piano and Dad plays his old French horn. He's teaching me some German polkas."

Leon had been eavesdropping. "You can get in a lot of trouble playing German polkas on a French horn, you know."

"Haven't you heard, Leon? The war's over."

I could tell Carl didn't get the joke, but there was no sense explaining it to him. Besides, there was some truth to Leon's remark. Speaking German or playing German music was a bad idea during the war. My parents and relatives only spoke German when we were upstairs in our apartment, never in the store.

Leon turned his attention to Carl. "How's your grandmother? She been baking any more of those éclairs lately?"

"She used up all her sugar-rationing coupons for last month. She's probably saving them up so she can bake a birthday cake for me tomorrow."

Leon leaned in closer. "So you're having a birthday party? You're inviting your scout and trick-or-treat buddies to your party, aren't you?"

Carl shrugged. "There's no party. Just me and Oma."

Leon kept at it. "You can't waste a whole cake on just you and your grandmother, Carl. You gotta have other kids there for a birthday party."

Carl hung his head.

"How many birthday parties have you had, Leon?"

I regretted my words the second they were out of my mouth. If it weren't for our family, Leon wouldn't have had a single birthday cake since his mother died.

Leon glared at me for a second, but the hope of cake brought him back fast. "I'll come to your party, Carl. Thanks for inviting me. What time do you want me to be there?"

"I don't know. Sometime in the afternoon, I guess. How about two o'clock?"

"I'll invite some of the other guys from the scout troop," Leon suggested.

"Don't you have to check with your grandma?" I asked.

"No, she won't mind. She'll be glad I've made friends since I moved here. You come, too, Norm." Carl was smiling now.

As Leon and I walked back to class I said, "Nothing like inviting yourself to a party that doesn't exist."

"Aw, c'mon. The poor kid doesn't have that many friends. Did you see how he perked up when I said I'd invite the other scouts? I figured it was my duty to help him celebrate his birthday."

"You just want to help him eat his cake."

"Well, sure. Somebody's gotta do it." Leon took off running down the hall. "Last one to class is a rotten egg," he called over his shoulder.

When I rounded the next corner, Leon was trying to talk the hall monitor out of making him stay after for running in the hall. I could tell by the expression on the monitor's face that Leon was winning, as usual.

——◆——

I had to work in the store in the morning. I told Mom about going over to Carl's house. "It's his birthday," I said.

Mom looked up from wiping the top of the meat counter. "Do you have a present to give him?"

"I drew some pictures after Jamboree. Maybe he'd like one of those."

"I just got in the Life Savers books for Christmas," Dad said. "They make good presents." Ellie and I each got one every year in our stockings. It was a box that hinged in the middle like a book, filled with rolls of Life Savers candy on each side.

"I think the picture sounds like a nicer gift," Mom said. "People like things that are made special for them."

I made a little mental note to draw pictures for my family for Christmas, which would be good, because I hadn't saved up much money. Dad would give me my allowance for doing nothing, but Mom insisted that I only get paid for the time I was actually working in the store.

As soon as I finished my work, I went upstairs and looked through the pictures I had drawn after Jamboree weekend. There was the one around the campfire where I had tried to show the way the fire glowed on everybody's face. I couldn't make it right with pencil, though. It just looked like all the faces had a three-day beard. Instead, I chose the drawing of the guys with their first-aid wounds. You could really tell who each kid was, especially Carl, with the bone sticking out of his arm. I rolled it up and put a rubber band around it.

Dad came upstairs for his lunch break with sandwiches for Ellie, himself, and me while Mom covered the store. He also brought a Life Savers book. "Why don't you take this to the boy, Norman? Can't have people thinking you're too cheap to buy a gift—especially when we have a family business."

"Okay, Dad." I made a mental note to start saving for Dad's Christmas present. Obviously he thought the only good gifts were the ones you bought.

The phone rang, and I grabbed it before Ellie did. It was Leon. "I can't go to Carl's today. Dad is taking me and Phyllis to Radio City to see *The Jolson Story*."

"You got the poor kid all keen on a party and now you're not going?"

"That's all the more cake for you." When I didn't say anything, he said in a low voice, "This is the first time Dad has wanted us to do something together in a long time, Norm. I gotta do it."

"Okay, I know."

There weren't many things that would keep Leon from connecting with a piece of cake, but I knew that spending time with his dad was one of them. I hoped maybe things would be looking up for Leon from now on.

"So who else is going?" I asked.

"Nobody. Just the three of us."

"Not to Radio City. I meant to Carl's party."

"Aw, nuts! I forgot to call anybody."

"You mean I'm the only one who knows about it?"

"Yeah, I guess so, unless Carl called some people."

"That's really rotten, Leon."

"I know. Listen, I gotta go. Dad's honking the horn."
He hung up before I could say anything else.

I got the phone book and slammed it down on the kitchen table.

"What are you so mad about?" Ellie asked. "That was Leon, wasn't it? Did you two have a fight?"

"None of your beeswax."

"Ellie asked you a question," Dad said. "That's no way to answer her."

"Aw, Leon was supposed to invite other guys from our troop to Carl's party, but he forgot. And now he's not even going himself because his dad is taking him and Phyllis to Radio City."

Ellie's eyes lit up. "Radio City Music Hall? Isn't the Christmas show on now with the Rockettes?"

"Yeah, I guess. All Leon said is the movie is *The Jolson Story*."

Ellie put her arms around Dad's neck. "Oh, could we go, Daddy? Could we go? Please?"

Dad poured himself a cup of coffee. "You'll have to ask your mother if she wants to. I'm too busy in the store this time of year."

"I'll ask her right now!" Ellie bolted from the table and ran downstairs.

For a while, the only sound in the kitchen was Dad sipping his coffee and me flipping through the phone book. I wrote down everybody's number, then called Bill and Gary, but nobody answered at either house. Ronnie was home, but he said he had farm work to do. That was the trouble with a pig farm. There were always chores to be done, even in the middle of winter.

When I called Charlie's number, I got the funeral home. That was creepy. Charlie's mother answered in this soft, sad-sounding voice. I guess you had to do that when your family owned a funeral home. When you owned a meat market, you could answer the phone in your normal voice. Anyway, Mrs. Ackerman said Charlie was off with his friends and she didn't know when he would be back. The only other person I could think of to call was Gordie Corrigan, but nobody could be desperate enough to want him at their party—not even Carl.

I put away the phone book. "Nobody can go to Carl's party. It's just me."

"It is pretty late notice," Dad said. "People are busy on Saturdays."

"I know."

I looked at the clock. It was one-thirty. I took another bite of my sandwich. Neither of us said anything for a few minutes, and then Dad broke the silence. "How are you getting along these days, Norman? Everything all right with you?"

"Yeah, mostly," I said. "I've been practicing baseball. Learning how to catch and throw with one hand, you know? I want to go out for the team this spring."

I saw Dad wince when I mentioned the hand. I thought he'd be over that by now. Then he rubbed his forehead. "Well, I don't think you should get your hopes up about the team, Norm. There are lots of other things in life besides baseball."

"I really think I can do it, Dad. I need to keep practicing how to get the mitt off and on faster so I can catch a ball, and then throw it. And I have to figure out how to make the ball go where I want it to when I bat. I need somebody to pitch to me or play catch."

I was waiting for Dad to say he'd do it, or at least give me some pointers, but he didn't. He just got up. "You'll find plenty to keep you busy without worrying about playing baseball."

"But, Dad . . ."

"Not now, Norman. I have to get back to the store."

My conversation with Dad made me lose my appetite, so after he left, I gave the rest of my sandwich to Knocky. I wasn't looking forward to this party. Oh, sure, the cake would be good, but it would be boring just sitting around with Carl and his grandmother. I thought about calling to tell him that something had come up. I even practiced a couple of excuses in my head, but each one ended with me telling him that nobody else was coming. After Leon got Carl all hepped up about a birthday party, I couldn't do that. I even thought about taking Ellie along so she could blabber on about stuff to Mrs. Oberndorfer, but I decided having Ellie there could be as bad as having Gordie.

I went outside to kill time practicing ball. I sure didn't want to get to Carl's early. Throwing the ball against the house wasn't much fun. I needed to be playing catch with another person. Carl was terrible at baseball, so it couldn't be him. If only Leon would help me practice ball instead of trying to convince me to take up a sport I could do with one hand—like running track. Leon could be a real pain sometimes, but I wished he was here now. Even with just him and me at Carl's party, we'd have a good time.

At ten of two, I put away my ball and glove, grabbed the birthday presents, and headed over to Carl's house.

Chapter 16

Carl answered the door. "Hi, Norm. You're the first one here."

Yeah, the first and the last, I thought.

"So where's Leon?" Carl asked. "I thought he would be coming with you."

"He had to go someplace with his dad." I didn't mention Radio City. Carl looked disappointed about it being only me. I didn't want to make him feel worse.

"That's okay. C'mon in."

His grandmother was setting the dining-room table, putting noisemakers on each plate. There were balloons and crepe-paper streamers hanging from the ceiling. She looked up and smiled. "Hello, Norman."

"Hello, Mrs. Oberndorfer."

"Call me Oma. Everybody does. Carl has been looking forward to his party."

"Yeah," Carl said. "Do you know who else is coming?"

"It's not going to be as many people as we thought."

Carl was still smiling. "We'll have a good time anyway. So who's coming?"

"Well, that's the thing," I said. "Nobody else was able to make it. People have lots of stuff to do on Saturdays." I didn't say Leon forgot to call them.

I could tell by the expression on Carl's face that he thought nobody came because they didn't like him. So much for not wanting Leon to look bad. "Listen, here's the truth, Carl. Leon's dad is taking him and his sister to New York today. Leon got so excited about it he forgot to call people about your party. He only told me an hour ago, so it was too late. All the guys would've come if they had known in time."

Mrs. Oberndorfer—Oma—had looked as disappointed as Carl, but she brightened up. "Those things happen. We'll have a fine party by ourselves."

"I almost forgot. Happy birthday, Carl." I handed him the Life Savers book and the drawing. I wished I had thought to wrap them in some birthday paper from the store, especially since Oma had gone to all the trouble of decorating.

"A Life Savers book. That's swell!" Carl put it on the table and started rolling the rubber band off the drawing. "What's this?"

"You'll see," I said. I almost added that it wasn't much of anything, but if he was only getting the two presents from me, I sure didn't want to run it down.

Carl smoothed the paper out on the table to take the roll out of it. "Wow, this is great, Norm. Did you draw it yourself?"

"Yeah."

"Look at this, Oma. It's me and the guys at Jamboree with the fake wounds Norm gave us. See?

164

Here's Bill with the knife stuck in his arm and Charlie with the fishhook poking out of his neck."

Oma pointed to the picture. "And there you are with your broken bone, Carl."

"Yeah, that's me all right."

"You're really quite an artist," Oma said. "You should sign this, though."

"Sign it?"

She handed me a pen. "All artists sign their work. Here, put it down in the corner."

I felt kind of stupid, but I signed my name.

"Put the date, too," Oma said. "That makes it official."

"This would be better in color," I said. "I need to get some paints."

Carl was still looking at the drawing. "I like it fine just like this."

Then Oma did the most amazing thing. She walked over to this picture on the wall and took it off the hook. "I think this frame is just about the right size." She took out the picture that was in it, replaced it with my drawing, and hung it on the wall. "There, how does that look?"

"It's perfect," Carl said.

"I never saw one of my drawings in a frame before."

"I think you'll be having a lot of your artwork framed in the future, Norm."

"That's right," Carl said. "He's going to be an artist when he grows up."

"Well, I don't know. I like to draw, is all."

"Norm is already an artist," Oma said. "Now, who's ready for some cake?"

I let Oma's words sink in. Mom used to put my drawings on the fridge when I was younger, but to have someone—not even a relative—take the trouble to put one into a frame and hang it on the wall for everybody to see, well, that was pretty special. Maybe I could get a real job as an artist when I grew up.

Oma came back with a chocolate cake topped with candles. The two of us sang "Happy Birthday" to Carl. I sang loud to make it sound like more people. Carl blew out all the candles in one breath.

Oma cut the cake, then dished up two huge bowls of chocolate ice cream for us and a small one for herself. All the talking stopped while we ate.

"That was the best chocolate cake I ever had," I said.

"Glad you enjoyed it. Carl, has Norm seen Opa's special project in the basement?"

"No, I wanted to show him and Leon on Halloween, but there wasn't time."

I started to follow Carl down the basement stairs, but he stopped me.

"Wait till I get things set up. It looks beautiful as you come down the stairs."

I could hear Carl moving around in the basement, but I couldn't see beyond the landing. I heard switches click and saw lights reflecting on the walls.

"Okay," Carl called. "Come on down."

I got to the landing and turned the corner. "Holy cow!"

Carl was in the middle of the biggest electric-train layout I had ever seen. It wrapped around him with only about a four-foot square space in the middle for standing at the controls, and an aisle so you could walk around the outside.

Carl grinned. "My Opa made most of it. I started helping him when I was old enough to handle the stuff without breaking it. Neat, huh?"

"I'll say! I mean, Dad and I have a train setup in the basement, but he just nailed the tracks down to a big board. We have a few houses and other buildings, and some of those dumb trees you can buy in a kit, but it's nothing like this. These trees look real, and how did you do the mountains and stuff?"

"It's chicken wire with papier mâché over it. Opa showed me how to paint the cliffs with shading to make them look real, instead of just using one color. Well, you know about stuff like that—you being an artist and all."

"Yeah, I guess, but I never thought of doing this with our train layout. With Dad and me, it's mostly about watching the train go around. We haven't even done much of that lately."

I walked around the whole layout, studying the way it was put together. It went through the four seasons. It was spring in the country, with animals in the field and blossoms on the trees in the orchard. For summer, it went into a small town with a circus setting up its tent. There was even a circus train with animal cages. "I've seen the circus train in the Lionel catalog, but I never saw anything like the tent being put up. Did that come in a kit?"

"No. Opa designed that himself. He sketched it out

the way he wanted it, then he made the people out of clay and the tent out of cloth from Oma's sewing. He had a sketch for a sideshow tent that had a fat lady, a sword swallower, and a snake charmer, but he didn't have a chance to finish them before he got sick. I tried to make them myself, but when I was done you couldn't tell what they were supposed to be."

"Where is your grandfather now? In the hospital?"

Carl shook his head. "He died last spring. Then in the summer Oma and I packed everything up and moved here."

"That's too bad," I said. "About your grandfather dying, I mean." I was going to ask Carl where his parents were, but I figured something bad must have happened to them, too, since he never mentioned them.

The next part of the layout was autumn in the mountains, with the trees all shades of red, yellow, and orange. The tracks went over a trestle high above a river and then wound down around the mountain. Then there was a town with snow and a lighted Christmas tree and a manger scene in the town square.

"Want to run the trains?" Carl asked.

"Are you kidding? Of course I want to run them."

Carl lifted a hinged section in the scenery so I could get to the center space. I liked the way he handed the controls right over to me. My cousin, Fred, showed me his train layout once, but he gave me a big lecture before he let me touch anything. Then he hovered over me the whole time like I was going to crash his precious Empire State Express into his California Zephyr. I almost wanted to do it just for spite. Carl wasn't like that. He just stepped back and let me take his New York Central 733 over the high trestle, without saying a word.

"So, Carl, if you moved here after your grandfather died, who set up the trains?"

Carl was watching the long freight go over the trestle with a big smile on his face. "I did."

"But what about all the electrical stuff?"

"I know how to do that. Opa taught me. And some of the scenery got banged up in the moving truck, so I had to patch it and repaint some things."

"You did a really nice job," I said.

Carl grinned. "Thanks."

We didn't talk much after that. We were too busy running all four of Carl's trains at once for the whole afternoon. It was the best birthday party I had ever been to.

Ellie convinced Mom to take us to Radio City the next weekend, which didn't surprise me. Mom was a lot easier on Ellie than she was on me. After the show, we went to Macy's to see the toys. The store windows had scenes of elves making toys in Santa's workshop. I wanted to take more time looking at them, but Ellie started whining about wanting to see the real toys in the store. We could hardly push through the mob of people on the first floor. We went up the big wooden escalators to the toy department. Right away, Ellie spotted the Margaret O'Brien doll and got all excited, since that was her favorite movie star.

I slipped away and hung out by the model-train

layout. It was nice, but nothing like the one Carl had in his basement. I couldn't wait to tell him his model-train setup was better than the one in the world's biggest department store.

They had a right-handed glove in the baseball display, but even though it was new, it wasn't as nice as mine. I left the sports section and headed over to the bicycles. There it was, my Raleigh three-speed racing bike. It looked really slick with its dark green paint, thin tires, and brakes on the handlebars. I couldn't wait to get my hands on it. I reached out to grip the handlebars, and it wasn't until my stump hit the left handle that I remembered. There were still times when it felt as if I had two hands. Like just then, I could feel the fingers of my left hand opening, ready to grip the handlebar.

A salesman came right over. "Is this beauty on your Christmas list, son?"

"Yes, sir. I've been wanting one of these. They go pretty fast, huh?"

"Oh, they're speedy, all right. Much faster than the balloon-tire bikes like the Columbias. And these have the double handlebar brakes instead of . . ." That's when he must have noticed my missing hand, because there was a flick of his eyes and his voice got syrupy. I hated when people did that. Why couldn't they just act normal? "Of course, there's nothing wrong with our fine line of Schwinns and Columbias. You might find them easier to handle."

Just then, Mom and Ellie came along. "Is this the bike you've been wanting, Norm?" Mom asked.

"I think another bike might be more suitable for him, ma'am."

"He's right, Mom. I couldn't work the handlebar brakes."

"You could work the one on the right side," Mom said.

The salesman looked embarrassed. "One brake isn't enough to stop him, ma'am. The brake on the right is for the front wheel. Using only the front brake would send him over the handlebars. The gearshift is on the left side, too."

Mom wasn't listening to him. She had found another challenge for me. "If you really want this bike, Norm, we can figure out a way to make it work."

"I don't care about the bike anymore!" I headed for the escalator before Mom could make a scene. She'd have me trying to ride the bike through the crowds in the toy department just to prove to the salesman that I could do it with one hand. With any luck at all, I'd slam on the right-handed brake, catapult over the handlebars, and wipe out the whole display of Margaret O'Brien dolls.

Mom didn't mention the bike on the ride home and neither did I. Ellie was babbling on about our day in New York, so neither of us got a word in edgewise.

I thought about that bike after I went to bed that night. It looked even better in person than it had in the pictures. The logo on the bike stem was a red *R* with a red bird head and gold trim. Last year, when I was plotting how to get my parents to buy it for me, I thought I'd have to convince them that it was worth spending the extra money because it was so much better than my old bike. It never occurred to me that I wouldn't get the bike because I couldn't ride it.

Most of the time I could forget about my hand. Well, not forget about it exactly, but I tried not to let it bother me. But that bike was different. I had dreamed about riding it. Now it was no use to me. For the first time in a long time, I cried myself to sleep.

Chapter 17

We had our first real snowstorm two days before Christmas. Up until then, we'd only had about an inch at a time. It would melt fast and I could get out to practice throwing and catching against the back wall. This time there were five or six inches, which put an end to practicing ball for a while. Dad didn't think there was enough snow to hire a guy to plow the parking lot, meaning I had to shovel it. I thought losing my hand would get me out of this job, especially since my stump was sensitive to the cold, but Mom found a way for me to work just as hard as I had with two hands. She knitted me a pair of mittens—one regular and the other with no thumb, tapered to fit my stump perfectly.

"It's good for you to get some exercise in the fresh air," Mom said.

"How about I just make a snowman and call it a day?"

When Mom gave me her look, I headed outside, armed with a shovel and the world's only green-and-red-striped stump mitten.

I tried lifting the shovel and tossing the snow to the side the way I used to do it, but that was too hard with one hand. I finally used the shovel like a plow and pushed it to the edges of the parking lot. At first it was still snowing, so it didn't seem like I was making much headway. Then the snow stopped and it got easier, at least until the cars started coming in. Almost everybody said something to me as they got out of their cars—mostly about how nice it was that we'd have a white Christmas. Yeah, right, unless you were in charge of keeping the white stuff out of the parking lot. I finally finished up and went into the store.

It was crowded with people coming in to get last-minute stuff for Christmas. Mom was sorting rationing stamps into little piles. "Looks like everybody saved their sugar rations for baking Christmas cookies. I hope we don't run out, the way we did last year."

"Do you have all the stuff for our cookies, Mom?"

"Don't worry, Norm. I made the cookie dough a couple of nights ago. It's in the icebox, ready to roll out." Mom sighed. "If I could get a few hours away from the store, I could get them baked, but we're much busier than usual."

Mom made the best Christmas cookies in the world. They had heavy cream and brandy in them. I got to thinking about those cookies and had an idea. I went into the back room to tell Dad.

"Mom hasn't had time to bake the cookies yet, so I'm going to do it for her as a Christmas present."

Dad pulled a dollar out of his pocket. "Run over to

the drugstore and buy your mother a real gift. Something nice. Maybe some perfume."

"Aw, Dad, Mom doesn't wear perfume. Besides, I know she's feeling bad about not baking the cookies. It would be a nice surprise for her."

"You don't know how to bake, Norm."

"Sure I do. Mom used to let me help her when I was a kid."

"She let you *think* you were helping. All you did was put the sugar sprinkles on the top. Rolling out the dough is the hard part. You have to get it really thin before you cut it."

"Okay, so I'll roll it out real thin. I can do it, Dad."

Dad shoved another bill at me. "Forget the cookies. Buy your mother something special. But first, give Mrs. Baumgartner some help with her turkey, will you?"

I knew Dad was pawning her off on me because she was a pain in the neck. I tried to force a smile. "How big a turkey do you want, Mrs. Baumgartner?"

She had her usual pickle-faced expression. "Well, at these black-market prices I can't get one anywhere near as big as I need. Twelve pounds will have to do."

"Coming right up, Mrs. Baumgartner." I went into the cooler, which was stacked with turkeys. I took off my mittens and hefted a bird. Both Mom and Dad could tell how much a turkey weighed by the feel of it in their hands. They could come within an ounce of the right weight. That never worked for me. I tried to do it by eye. I took the turkey out into the store and put it on the scale.

"Fifteen and a half pounds!" yelled Mrs. Baumgartner. "Are you trying to rob an old woman blind? Why don't you just beat me up and steal my purse?"

Dad looked over at us. "It's not easy to judge the weight of a turkey, Mrs. Baumgartner. Give the boy a chance. He'll find the perfect bird for you."

"I don't have all day to be standing around," Mrs. Baumgartner said. "It's not my job to let Norman practice on my turkey."

Dad was with another customer, so he didn't say anything. I went back into the cooler and found a smaller one. This time the needle barely passed ten pounds.

"I'm supposed to feed my whole family on that scrawny bird? You want I should starve my family?"

I took that turkey back and made one last try. At least now I knew what too big and too small looked like, so I found a turkey that was in between. It came up as twelve pounds two ounces. "There," I said. "How's this one?"

She shook her finger at me. "You went over the weight to squeeze an extra nickel out of an old woman."

"I'm sorry, Mrs. Baumgartner. I'll try again if you want."

"Do I look like someone who has all day to wait around for the butcher's son to find the right-sized turkey for me? I'll take this one."

Dad called over to us. "I'll wrap that up for you, Mrs. Baumgartner."

"If I were you, Walter Schmidt, I'd have that boy practice weighing turkeys when the store is closed, so he doesn't waste your customers' time."

"Nice bird Norm found for you, Mrs. Baumgartner. Should make a fine Christmas dinner."

When I put the turkey on the meat counter, Mrs. Baumgartner grabbed my left arm. "That hand hasn't grown back yet? It hasn't even started to sprout?"

I didn't know what to say, but Dad spoke up. "The hand won't grow back, Mrs. Baumgartner. It doesn't work that way."

"I'm sure I've read about that happening," Mrs. Baumgartner insisted. "My daughter says even starfish can grow new arms when one gets cut off."

"That's starfish, not people," Dad said. "It's not the same thing."

I was surprised Dad was bothering to correct Mrs. Baumgartner. He usually just let her go on about things. But I could tell Mrs. Baumgartner was getting his goat. His face was red and his mouth was set in a tight line.

Mrs. Baumgartner sniffed and stuck her nose in the air. "I know what I know, Walter Schmidt." She gave my arm a squeeze. "And you, young man, be vigilant. One of these days you'll wake up and see the tiny bud of a new hand."

"Yes, ma'am, I'll keep watching for that, all right." I slipped out of Mrs. Baumgartner's grip and made my escape out of the store. I sure was glad I wasn't going to be taking over the business when I grew up. Store owners had to put up with a lot of crazy people, and I didn't have the patience for it.

Nobody was in the apartment, so this was my chance to make the Christmas cookies. I pulled out Mom's rolling pin and board and found the bowl of cookie dough in the icebox. I broke off a chunk of dough and started rolling. I thought it might be hard to do it with one hand, but I could press down on the left handle of the rolling pin with my stump, so it was no problem. I rolled until I could see the wood grain of the board through the dough.

Then I took a star-shaped cookie cutter and pressed it down. When I lifted the cutter, the dough didn't come with it the way it did when Mom made cookies. What had I done wrong? I took a spatula and tried to pry up the star. I finally got it loose, but it was all twisted out of shape, and one of the points was missing. "Try and grow back *that* arm, starfish," I mumbled.

Then I remembered Mom punching the dough and rolling it around on the board with her hands. That was what went wrong. I scraped up the whole mess and rolled it into a ball, which wasn't easy, because it stuck to my hand something fierce. I held the spatula under my left arm to scrape the dough off my hand. Finally I gave up and chewed off the dough that stuck between my fingers.

I pounded down the lump of dough, then flattened it with my hands. This time I would only need to use the rolling pin a little bit, because the stuff was already stretched thin. I ran the rolling pin over the dough and came out with a perfect dough-covered rolling pin.

So now I scraped everything off the rolling pin, then used a second spatula to get the dough off the first spatula. This was tricky to do with one hand. I licked off what I missed with the spatula. I made the dough into a ball, and pounded the daylights out of it. This time when I tried to roll it out, the dough stuck to everything it touched.

That's when I read Mom's recipe to see if there were any special instructions. There was nothing that gave me a clue why I was making such a mess. I didn't want to ask Mom and spoil her surprise, and I sure wasn't going to ask Dad. I decided to call Oma for advice, since she was such a good baker.

Carl was the one who answered the phone. I told him my problem.

"Oma won't be home until suppertime. I've watched her bake cookies lots of times, though. You want me to come over and help?"

"Sure."

Carl showed up about ten minutes later. He knew a lot about baking cookies. He knew that you had to sprinkle flour on the board before you rolled out the cookies so they wouldn't stick.

"I can't believe they didn't say that in the recipe."

"They did. Right before the part about handling the dough as little as possible."

"But what about punching it down and pushing it around with your hands? I know I've seen Mom do that."

"That's for bread, not for cookies."

"Oh."

"You have any more of this cookie dough?"

"I put the rest back in the icebox." I got the bowl and set it on the table.

Carl looked at it. "I thought so."

"What?"

"I was pretty sure your mother's cookie dough wasn't supposed to be gray. Did you wash your hands—hand—before you started this?"

"Well, sort of. I've been licking off the dough, so my hand is pretty clean."

Carl rolled his eyes, then went over to the sink to wash his hands and made me do the same.

"I don't know what the big deal is," I mumbled. "The gray color will be covered up with the colored sugar."

"Sprinkle some flour on the board," Carl said. "Not too much, though, or you'll make the cookies tough." I wanted to eat a piece of cookie dough, but Carl stopped me. "Wait until the end. You already wrecked some of the dough, so let's see how many cookies we get before you eat any."

We set up an assembly line. He did the cutting, I did the decorating with colored sugar and put them in the oven, then he took the baked cookies off the pan and I greased the pan for the next batch. After a while we switched jobs so we wouldn't get bored. We had it timed like clockwork, with a pan of cookies coming out of the oven every ten minutes. By five o'clock we had all the cookies baked, cooled, and packed up in Mom's Christmas cookie tins. We even opened the window and fanned the air to get rid of the telltale cookie smell.

We finally got to eat the last of the cookie dough. "This is almost better than the baked cookies," I said.

Carl nodded. "I know. When Oma bakes chocolate chip cookies, we cut up little pieces of the dough and mix them into vanilla ice cream."

"What a great idea! I bet you could make a million dollars if you sold that."

Carl looked at the clock. "I'd better get home. It's almost dinnertime."

"Okay. Thanks for helping me out. This is going to be a great surprise for Mom. I owe you a favor."

Carl grinned. "Give me a couple of cookies and we'll call it even."

As Carl was running down the stairs, I thought about how different it would have been if Leon had been the one helping me with the baking. Between eating the cookie dough, which was one of his favorite things, and munching on the baked cookies, we'd be lucky to have half a tin. We would have had a lot of laughs, though.

Carl had only been gone a few minutes when I heard Mom coming up the stairs. She was moving slow, so I could tell she was tired.

She sat to rub her feet before starting dinner. "It's good to have so much business, but I'm glad Christmas Eve is tomorrow. I'm exhausted."

When she washed her hands in the sink, I took a peek to make sure we hadn't left any scraps of cookie dough. We hadn't. Carl must have cleaned it up.

Ellie came in with the new *Life* magazine. "Mommy! Here's a picture of Macy's from last weekend. I think we're in it."

She opened the magazine on the table. There was

a full-page picture taken from the second floor show-ing the escalator and the first floor. It looked like a swarm of ants. "I think that's us on the escalator," she said, pointing. "There's Mommy's hat, and the person next to her is me."

"The dot next to her, you mean," I said. "Besides, there are millions of people living in New York, not counting ones who come in to shop. Why would the *Life* photographer take the picture just as you're going up the escalator?"

Ellie snatched back the magazine. "It could hap-pen. I'm going to tell all my friends that I'm in *Life*. And I'm going to put this picture up on my wall."

Mom told us at dinner that we wouldn't have cookies for Christmas Eve. "We have some good pack-aged cookies in the store."

"But they're not the same, Mommy," Ellie whined.

"A person can only do so much," Dad said. "When you have a business like ours, the holidays get busy and the family has to sacrifice. Your mother's cookies would taste as good at Easter as they do at Christmas."

"You're not going to make them until *Easter*?" Ellie screeched.

"Your father is just making a point. I'll make them sometime next week."

I had to smile at Dad's comment. Every year Mom packed a special red tin of cookies just for Dad. They always disappeared right after Christmas Eve. I thought he ate them right away. Then last year, around the middle of March, Dad went into the back corner of the meat cooler and came out munching on something.

At first I thought he was gnawing on a piece of raw meat, because one of his favorite things is steak tartare—raw beef that you eat with raw eggs and horseradish. If you have it on New Year's Eve, it's supposed to bring you luck all year. I was never keen on steak tartare, but after the meat-grinder incident, I didn't even want to look at it.

Anyway, when Dad walked by me, I could hear crunching as he chewed. I knew raw beef didn't crunch, so I slipped into the cooler and found the round red tin with a picture of Santa Claus on the top. There were about a dozen cookies inside. I almost took one, but then I thought if Dad had made those cookies last for three months, he knew exactly how many he had left. I took a good long sniff, then closed the box, and put it away.

I never let on about Dad's secret. I figured that some day, when there were still enough cookies in the tin so they'd be hard to count, I might sneak one. A Christmas cookie around the middle of February would sure hit the spot.

Chapter 18

*D*ad closed the store at five on Christmas Eve, and we all went over to the Happy Valley for dinner so Mom didn't have to cook. We did that every year. Usually Leon came with us, but when I called to invite him this year, he said his family was going to spend Christmas with some cousins in Connecticut.

"Okay. Well, I'll see you when you get back."

"Sure," Leon said. "Merry Christmas."

"Yeah, you too."

When we went into the Happy Valley, it smelled wonderful. The Schneiders specialized in German food, which Dad said reminded him of home. They always closed their restaurant early on Christmas Eve, and we got to eat any dishes that hadn't sold that day. They had everything spread out on a long table.

"Ah, the rest of the family is here," Mr. Schneider said, coming over to greet us. We weren't related, but our families had been friends for a long time.

Dad shook his hand. "I've been looking forward to your delicious sauerbraten all day, Gene. You got any left?"

"Sure do. It's made from that fine Schmidt beef, so it's bound to be good."

Dad stood and talked business with Mr. Schneider for a few minutes while we joined Mrs. Schneider and the girls at the family table. They started passing bowls and platters around. I took some Wiener schnitzel, the little noodles called spaetzle, and a couple of bratwursts. Dad settled in with his plate of sauerbraten, and Mrs. Schneider poured Rhine wine for everybody. Even the kids got to have some. German polkas were playing on the jukebox. All through the war, Mr. Schneider never hid the fact that he was German. He served mostly German food and had a sign that said *Frohe Weihnachten* instead of Merry Christmas.

I could tell by the happy look on Dad's face that he felt like he was back in the old country again. I was having a good time, too, but it seemed funny not having Leon with us. He had stayed over with us every Christmas Eve since his mother died.

Once, I said it was sad that Leon didn't have Christmas with his own family. "The holidays are hard for people who have lost a loved one," Dad had said. "Leon is better off with us until Christmas is over."

I was glad that things were looking up for Leon's family now, but it meant I didn't see as much of him as before.

Ellie couldn't sit still all through dinner. "Can't we skip dessert and go home to open our presents?" she whispered to Mom.

Mrs. Schneider overheard her and laughed. "That's

186

the first time I heard you want to pass up dessert, Ellie. Don't you want my Christmas stollen?"

"I'm sure she does," Mom said. "Besides, we can't get home too early. We have to give Santa time to leave your presents."

Ellie rolled her eyes. "Oh, Mommy."

I wasn't sure if Ellie still believed in Santa or not. I never let my parents know when I stopped believing. I was afraid they'd be more disappointed than I was. They always made us sit facing the opposite side of the restaurant from our apartment so we couldn't look out and see Santa's sleigh on our roof. When we'd leave the house, the only gifts under the tree were the ones we had wrapped for each other. When we'd get back from dinner, there would be a few special unwrapped presents for Ellie and me. I never figured out how the gifts got there. It could have been our uncle, or maybe Dad had Ray do it. Even though I never found out who our Santa was, I was way younger than Ellie when I decided it wasn't some guy in a red suit with a bunch of reindeer.

Ellie practically made us choke down our cake so we could get home. Everybody thought it was cute that she still believed in Santa, so she didn't get yelled at. If I had pulled that trick, it would have been a different story.

Ellie was all the way up the stairs by the time the rest of us got across the parking lot. "She's here!" Ellie shrieked. "Santa left me my Margaret O'Brien!"

I don't know why she was so surprised. I couldn't remember a single Christmas when Ellie didn't get what she asked for—well, except for the year she wanted a live kangaroo. I wasn't that excited about Christmas. Usually there was one thing I was hoping for, but this year I hadn't dropped a hint. I had thought about asking for a new baseball bat, but my old one was still good, and I didn't need a ball or glove. The only thing I had really wanted was my dream bike. Once I knew I couldn't have that, nothing else mattered.

When we got upstairs, I saw that there wasn't an unwrapped Santa gift for me. Mom and Dad never had any presents from Santa either, so I figured this was the year I was supposed to turn into an adult. From what I'd seen so far, being an adult wasn't all that much fun. Dad switched on the tree lights and the ones in our Christmas village on the mantel. The village reminded me of Carl's train layout. I wished I had made some stuff for our train to surprise Dad. Instead I had just bought him a new tie—the most boring gift a kid could give to his dad.

Mom went into the kitchen and came out with a plate of Christmas cookies from the store. Just looking at them, you could tell they wouldn't taste as good as hers. They were three times as thick, and paste-white instead of golden brown. Mom passed the plate to Dad, but he waved them away. "No, thanks. I'll wait for the real thing."

Ellie was too busy mooning over her doll to want cookies. Mom held out the plate to me. "No, thanks."

"Nobody in this house ever turns down cookies," Mom said. "These are perfectly good. Just try one."

"I'm stuffed, Mom. Did you see how much I ate at

the Schneiders'? I had three bratwursts and two Wiener schnitzels."

Mom sighed and sat down on the couch. She reached under the tree and handed everybody a present. Mine was socks. I didn't even try to act excited about them because I'm not that good an actor.

Dad opened my tie. He made a big fuss over it. "Now that's what I call a nice gift, Norm. I'll save this for special occasions."

Mom opened the present I had bought for her. I got bath powder because I knew she didn't wear perfume, but everybody has to take baths. She sniffed it and said how much she liked it. Dad nodded his approval.

I opened another package—a pair of hand-knitted mittens from Mom. "Great, Mom. Now if it snows right after I finish shoveling, I'll have dry mittens to go right out again."

Mom looked hurt. "They're not just for shoveling, Norm. You and Leon like to do other things in the winter, like sledding and skating."

I felt bad because she had gone to the trouble of making them. "I know, Mom. I was only kidding. They're great, honest! Thanks." Now I wished I had asked for a bat or baseball after all. At least I'd have something I could play with instead of all stuff to wear.

Mom had knitted Ellie a sweater and a matching one for her doll. Ellie practically popped her cork over that. "Margaret O'Brien and I can dress just alike!"

"There's another present under the tree for you, Norm," Dad said. "See the one with the red wrapping paper?"

I pulled it out and shook it. Some stuff was rattling around inside, which was a good sign. It couldn't be more mittens or socks. Dad had a big grin on his face. "Santa said you've been wanting this."

"Oh yeah?" I ripped at the paper. "How did he know? I didn't send him a letter."

"Santa knows everything," Ellie said. "He sees you when you're sleeping. He knows if you're—"

"I know, I KNOW!" Boy, if there was one Christmas song I hated it was that one. Just the thought of some old guy with a beard watching every move I made gave me the creeps. I pulled off the last of the paper to find a wooden box. Then I lifted the lid. "Holy cow! It's a set of oil paints." The box was filled with little tubes of paint and had a special section with some brushes. There were three canvas boards and a book about painting to go with it.

"Well, if you're going to be an artist, you need to have the right supplies," Dad said. "There's turpentine to clean up with and linseed oil for something or other. I didn't put them in the box, but the guy at the store said you'd need them. The book tells you how to mix the colors."

"Thanks, Dad. This is just what I've always wanted." I couldn't believe that Dad had bought this for me, especially with him feeling the way he did about me being an artist. I opened each tube to smell the paint and see if the color was really the same as the stripe on the outside.

I don't know how long I had been fooling around with my paints when I heard Mom say, "It's been a long day. I think I'll turn in for the night."

"Okay," I said, barely looking.

"Ellie, it's time for bed. You can play with your doll in the morning."

Mom came over and gave me a kiss on the cheek. "Don't stay up too late, Norm. And thanks for my nice powder. Merry Christmas."

That's when I remembered. "Wait! There's another present."

"It can wait until morning," Dad said.

"No! It can't!" I ran to the kitchen and took the cookie tins out of the broom closet, where I had hidden them. "Everybody sit down and close your eyes, because they're not wrapped."

When I walked into the room with the three tins, Mom, Dad, and Ellie all had their eyes closed. I could tell Ellie was peeking through her squinty eyes. I was going to give all three tins to Mom, but I changed my mind at the last second. I put two on her lap, and I handed the red one with the Santa Claus picture to Dad. "I know you don't like homemade presents, Dad, but I think this is different. Okay, you can look now."

"What's this?" Mom said.

"Open it up, Mom."

"My cookies? You baked them, Norm?"

Dad had taken one out of his tin. "Nice and thin and browned just the way I like them." He took a bite. "Perfect."

Mom opened her tin and looked up at me. "When did you do this?"

"Yesterday. Carl helped."

"Eeeuw," Ellie said. "Boys can't make cookies."

Mom took a bite of cookie. "Delicious. I couldn't have made them better myself."

Ellie grabbed one and ran to her room with it. She wouldn't give me the satisfaction of eating it in front of me.

Mom gave me a big hug before she went to bed. "That's the nicest Christmas surprise I ever got, Norm."

"Me, too." Dad was clutching his red tin. "Who says I don't like homemade gifts?"

The next morning at breakfast, Mom and Dad were smiling at each other when they thought I wasn't looking. "What's going on with you guys?" I asked. "Why are you acting all happy?"

"It's Christmas," Mom said. "We're supposed to be happy."

"Well, I'm happy," Ellie said. "I'm going over to Ginny's house. We're going to play with our Margaret O'Brien dolls."

"You both got the same doll?" I said. "That's dumb."

"It is not. It's what we both wanted. So there!" She flounced out of the room.

Just then the doorbell rang. "Hey, Norm!" Leon yelled up the stairs. "Come down and see what I got for Christmas!"

"How come you're back so soon?"

"Dad wanted to come home so he could give me my Christmas present. It was too big to take with us."

"What is it?"

"I'm not telling. You gotta come down to see it."

I grabbed my jacket and ran down the stairs.

"Is this swell or what?"

I couldn't believe my eyes. Leon had my bike. Just exactly the one I wanted, with the thin wheels, green paint, and brakes on the handlebars.

"I asked Dad for it, but I never thought he'd get it for me," he said.

"That's great, Leon." As much as I wanted to be happy for him, I was really peeved that Leon got the bike I had picked out. He had never even heard of a Raleigh racing bike until I showed him the picture. There were all kinds of bikes in the stores. He had some nerve asking for the same one I wanted.

"It's the best present I ever got in my whole life, Norm. Dad got some nice stuff for Phyllis, too. Did I tell you he has a regular job now?"

Leon looked so happy, I felt sort of guilty for being jealous about the bike. He usually didn't get much for Christmas. This bike was a bigger deal for him than it would've been for me. Besides, I got my oil paints, so I couldn't complain.

Mom, Dad, and Ellie had followed me downstairs.

"That's a nice-looking bike, Leon," Dad said.

Mom handed me my new mittens and a hat. "You two ought to go for a ride to try it out. The roads are clear of snow."

I wasn't so keen on riding my old clunker with Leon on the new Raleigh, but I'd have to do it sooner or later, so I figured I might as well get it over with. Besides, Leon would do the same for me if it were the other way around. "Okay. I'll get my bike."

Leon got off his bike and leaned it toward me.

"Here, try mine out, Norm. I've been riding it all over the neighborhood. I'll ride yours for a while."

I was tempted, but I shook my head. I could see myself crashing his new bike because I couldn't work the brakes. "Don't be stupid, Leon. You gotta ride your new bike on Christmas Day. I'll try it out some other time."

Then, when I opened our garage door, I saw it. My old clunker was gone, and there in its place was my dream bike—just like Leon's.

Dad was standing outside the garage door, grinning. "Moving both brakes to the right side was your mother's idea. You can operate them together with your right hand, see?" Dad grasped both brakes at the same time. "Clever woman, your mother."

I ran my fingers over the Raleigh logo on the bike stem. "I can't believe you got me this."

"I can't believe you and Leon both got the same present," Ellie said. "That's so dumb."

"It is not!" I said. "It's what we both wanted. So there!"

With that, Leon and I took off on our Raleigh three-speed racing bikes with their slick dark green paint, thin tires, and brakes on the handlebars.

Life was good.

Chapter **19**

We didn't get much snow after that Christmas storm, so we rode our bikes a lot. It didn't take me any time at all to get used to working both brakes with my right hand. The bikes went like the wind. We'd race all the way down Chauncey, where we didn't have to worry about traffic.

The snow didn't melt in our back yard, because it was shady most of the day. I couldn't practice catching and throwing, but I shoveled out a spot to work on my batting. It was still hard to tell if I was hitting the ball high or low, because the ball swung back and forth in the arc made by the rope. I figured I needed something that would stretch when I hit the ball. I found a spring in the garage, cut the rope, and tied the spring into it about five inches from the ball.

It did what I thought it would. When I hit the ball, the spring stretched, giving the ball enough leeway to go off in a straight line. The only problem was that the spring made the ball zing back at me like a bullet. I never even saw it coming. It caught me on the side of the head, knocking me down. I could almost see little birds twittering around my head like in the cartoons.

When I hit the second time, I got the bat in position to swing again right away. What had seemed to be a problem turned into a good thing. It forced me to really keep my eye on the ball, because it could be coming at me from any angle. I could swing at twice the number of balls I would get if I had somebody pitching to me. I learned to react fast and get much more accurate with my swing. And now I could tell if I was hitting a grounder or a high fly to the outfield.

It got dark early in the winter, so that cut short the baseball practice and bike rides. That's when I'd go inside to mess around with my new oil paints. I loved the way they smelled and the way I could blend colors. The first thing I tried painting was my idea of how the new cars would look. I made a red one with pointy fenders and a glass windshield that curved around the sides of the car instead of the two flat pieces of glass with a bar of metal down the middle like our car had. I put plenty of chrome on it, too. It was hard to figure out how to paint something that was shiny silver until I used Mom's silver vase as a model.

"Mom's going to yell at you for taking her good vase out of the china cabinet," Ellie said. She was always sticking her nose into my room.

Mom had been coming up the stairs and must have heard Ellie, because she came in to see what kind of trouble I was getting into.

"I'm not getting paint on your vase, Mom."

Mom looked at my painting. "That's very good. You have an artist's eye."

"I have two of them," I said, "which is twice as good as my hand situation. Of course there was van Gogh, who had only the one ear."

Mom grinned and gave me a light smack on the side of the head. "I'm going to start dinner, so be cleaned up in half an hour."

I couldn't get the curved-glass windshield right, then I remembered I had saved a *Life* magazine that had a picture of an experimental car with a curved Plexiglas top. I searched through my closet and under the bed for the magazine but couldn't find it in my room. I looked through the pile of magazines in the living room, but it wasn't there either. All the other issues were still there, so it had to be around somewhere.

"Has anybody seen the November *Life* I was saving?" I asked at dinner.

"If it's the one with the Margaret O'Brien ad, it's mine," Ellie said.

I remembered the ad for radios with Margaret O'Brien's picture. I should have known Ellie would go for that. "I need that magazine," I said.

"I need it, too. I'm collecting Margaret O'Brien pictures. You can't have it."

"Stop arguing," Mom said. "Each of you can cut out the pictures you want."

After dinner I worked on my windshield using the picture. Turns out it didn't help me that much because the picture was in black and white, but I learned that glass has light and dark streaks. By the time I finished, it looked pretty true to life.

In the next few days, I painted a couple more cars, this time with mountains and trees in the background. It was less than a week after Christmas and I had used up all my canvases. Then I read in the painting book that you could paint on cardboard if you coated it first. You were supposed to get gesso, but I just used some old blue trim paint Dad had in the garage, and it worked fine. It made the paintings more interesting to have the dark blue background anyway. That's when I tried doing the campfire from Jamboree. I made the light on the faces look exactly the way I had seen it.

Over the next few weeks I followed this up with some paintings of my favorite baseball players. Now that I could use cardboard, I had an unlimited supply of canvases. My room was starting to look like an art gallery. It smelled like turpentine, which I loved, even though Ellie complained that it stunk. That made me like the smell even more, because it kept her out of my stuff.

I had used up more than half my paint tubes. Mom was always yelling at me because I squeezed toothpaste from the middle, but with the paints, I rolled them up from the bottom, flattening them with my scout knife to force out the last possible drop. Finally, I was left with colors like yellow ochre, viridian, and raw sienna, which made for some strange-looking paintings. I'd have to save up for some new paint.

Pretty soon it was spring. Not the time of spring where you had birds and flowers. It was February—time for spring training. Baseball was back in action! I searched every magazine and sports section to find news of the Giants. They were training in Arizona this year instead of Florida. The Cleveland Indians were there, too, so I was always on the lookout for exhibition games on the radio. I was listening for any tip that would help me be a better player. I was still practicing my heart out in the back yard. It wouldn't be long before I'd get to play baseball for real again, and this time I'd be ready.

Around the end of the month, Dad said he was going over to the Chevy dealer in Danbury to take a look at the new cars.

"Can I go with you, Dad? I've been waiting to see those new models."

"You were disappointed last year, Norm," Mom said. "They didn't look any different than the cars before the war."

"I know, but they've had a whole year to come up with new designs. I know what they're going to look like." I ran into my room and came back with my car paintings and drawings.

Mom looked over my shoulder. "Those are a little snazzy for my taste. I don't care about moving fast. I just want a car that can get me to Danbury and back without breaking down."

"But a car should be exciting," I said.

Mom raised her eyebrows. "Seems to me you've had enough excitement with cars to last a lifetime."

Why did she keep bringing that up? When I was about six, I had gone on a delivery run with Al, an old guy who didn't mind me hanging around. When Al backed his truck up to the rear entrance of our store and got out, I slid over to the driver's seat. Al had left the keys in the truck. As he went into the store, I turned the key. Nothing happened.

"Hey, Al," I asked when he came back outside. "How you do to start the truck? Just turn the key?"

"No, you have to push in the clutch at the same time, but don't you go messing with it, hear?"

That was important information—something I hadn't picked up from watching people drive. I knew where the clutch was, though. If I stood up, I could reach the clutch pedal and see out of the front windshield at the same time. I checked to make sure Al wasn't around, and then jammed the pedal to the floor while I turned the key. Not only did the truck start, but it moved—fast! Backward! It stopped fast, too, right up against the back of the store, after it knocked out the post supporting the upstairs porch.

I was trying to figure out how to make the truck go forward so nobody would know what happened when everybody came piling out of the store—even the customers.

Dad and Al had this big argument while they sized up the damage. Mom didn't get into the argument. After she checked to make sure I wasn't hurt, she grabbed me by the ear, took me into the garage, and gave me the worst licking of my life. In the end, Al helped Dad repair the porch and Dad helped Al pull the dent out of his bumper. But from then on, Al wouldn't take me along on delivery runs.

Even that incident hadn't made me lose my love for cars, though. I was counting down the days until I could get my driver's permit. Only four years, three months, and two days to go.

"Hey, Dad," I said, trying to get Mom's mind off the truck disaster, "can Leon come with us to the Chevy place?"

"I don't remember saying *you* could come with me. Now you want me to drag Leon along, too?"

"Sure. I'll call him, okay?"

Dad sighed. "All right. But I'm leaving as soon as you get home from school. If either of you has to stay after, I'm going without you."

When I called Leon, he wanted to come right over and look at my car paintings again. We had the pictures all spread out on the kitchen table when the doorbell rang. It was Carl.

"Come on up," I yelled. "We're designing new cars."

Carl took the stairs two at a time. "Are we supposed to do this for school?"

"No. Norm's dad is taking us to see the new Chevies tomorrow," Leon said. "We're trying to guess what they'll look like."

Carl picked up one of my paintings. "This is nice, but I bet they'll look just like they did last year."

"That's how much you know," Leon said. "They have to make them really sharp so people will want to buy them."

"People are dying to buy new cars," Carl said. "Their old ones are falling apart. I bet there won't be enough new ones to go around."

"I think the car makers are going to want the new models to look special," I said. "They've had a whole year to design something great."

"It's not just designing them," Carl said. "They need to retool the plants. They've been making army stuff. It's hard enough to change the assembly line to make the old-style cars. They haven't had time to gear up for a different model."

Leon stepped between Carl and me. "You think you're so smart, Carl, but we'll show you. When Norm and I come home from the dealer, we'll bring you a picture of the new cars. Better yet, maybe Norm's dad will buy one and we'll drive home in it. And I bet it'll have fenders even pointier than these. So there."

It bothered me that Leon was being nasty to Carl. I felt funny not inviting him to go along with us, but I didn't say anything. That's when Dad came upstairs for a coffee break.

"You boys still going on about cars?"

"Yes, sir, Mr. Schmidt," Leon said. "I'm really looking forward to seeing the new models tomorrow."

Dad smiled. "I suppose you're coming along now, too, right, Carl?"

"I sure would like to, Mr. Schmidt."

"Fine," Dad said. "Just make sure you're here right after school."

"Pretty soon we'll be taking the whole scout troop," Leon said. "I'll see you later. I gotta get home." He ran down the stairs and slammed the door.

"What's eating him?" Dad said.

I just shrugged, but I knew he was sore about having Carl horn in on the car trip.

I could hardly wait for school to be out the next day. We all piled into our old car and took off. The car seemed to know we were getting rid of it, because it didn't stall once all the way to Danbury. When Dad pulled into the dealership, Carl, Leon, and I all took off running for the showroom.

"You kids behave yourselves or you'll stay outside," Dad called. We slowed down a little bit, but each of us wanted to be the first to catch a glimpse of the cars. When I saw them, I couldn't believe my eyes. "What the . . . what have the Chevy people been doing all year? These are just the same old thing."

"I told you so. Retooling. That's the problem." Carl was walking slowly around a blue four-door sedan. "They moved the parking lights below the headlights. That's new, and so is the ornament above the grille."

Leon was steamed. "Okay, Mr. Car Design expert. Maybe moving some lights and putting a doodad on the hood is a big deal to you, but it's the same stupid car. The fenders are as round as a pig's rear end."

A salesman came over just in time to hear Leon's comment. "If you boys aren't here with your parents, you'll have to leave."

Dad caught up with us. "They're with me. I'm looking for a coupe."

The salesman got over being annoyed at Leon and started giving Dad the sales pitch on a baby blue coupe. When he opened the door, I stuck my head inside and took a big whiff. It may have looked like an old car, but it sure smelled new. They should figure out a way to bottle up that smell so people could spray it inside their old cars.

"Try out those deeply cushioned seats and the luxurious upholstery, sir," the salesman said. "You won't find that quality in any of our competitors' cars."

Dad got behind the wheel. He wasn't talking. He always said when somebody is trying to sell you something you should keep your mouth shut and let him think you aren't impressed.

"The back seat has plenty of room for your whole family," the salesman continued. "Let's see how your three sons fit in there."

We all dove into the back seat. The seats were real cushy. "Boy, there's nothing like a new car, is there?" I said. Then I saw Dad giving me the evil eye through the rearview mirror. "I'm not sure I like the color, though," I added, just so the guy wouldn't think I was keen on it.

"Me and my brothers here like red," Leon said. "You have any red cars?"

I tried not to laugh, but I snorted, and then all three of us cracked up. Dad got out of the car and held the door open. "I warned you all before. Now you'll wait outside."

"But, Dad . . ."

"No buts. You've seen the cars. Get out of here while I talk business."

We watched through the showroom window.

"You think he's going to buy it?" Carl asked.

"I can't tell. He's got his poker face on."

There was a lot of head shaking and hand waving between Dad and the salesman. Then all of a sudden Dad was nodding his head. The guy went to the phone and came back to Dad. Then they shook hands.

"He's buying it!" Leon said. "They just made a deal."

We ran to meet Dad at the door. "You got the car?" I asked.

"Not that one," Dad said.

"Which one? The four-door?"

The salesman came outside. "Just follow me, Walter. It's about a twenty-minute drive."

"All right, Sam. I'll be right behind you."

We piled into our car. "Does he have another dealership, Dad?"

"No, he has a good used car that belongs to one of his relatives. It's a '37 Ford with only four thousand miles on it."

"A '37! That's older than our car. And you always get Chevies."

"It's a good deal," Dad said. "His aunt was only eligible for an 'A' gas-ration sticker during the war. She figured she could drive so little, it wasn't worth keeping the car on the road, so she had it put up on blocks in her garage to preserve the tires. Now she feels she's too old to drive."

"Wait a minute," I said. "This car belonged to some old lady?"

"That's right. And now it will belong to us."

Leon had practically slid off the seat laughing. "This isn't funny," I hissed.

"Oh, yes it is."

I wasn't ready to give up. "Are you sure you don't want a new car, Dad?"

"I'm sure I don't want to pay fourteen hundred dollars for one. This will be a good reliable car and it won't break the bank."

I was miserable. It was bad enough that the new cars weren't as special as I had wanted them to be, but at least they were shiny and new. And they hadn't belonged to some little old lady. We pulled up to a house on the outskirts of Lake Carmel. Sam jumped out and went to the door. The person who answered was Mrs. Baumgartner. Even Dad groaned when he saw her.

"I guess the shoe is on the other foot, now, isn't it, Walter?" she said. "I'm the one with something to sell to you. Maybe I should push my price up the way you charge black-market prices for your meat."

I didn't even go look at the car while Sam and Dad took it down off the blocks. Then Dad started it up and drove it down the road and back.

"Don't you be using up all my gas, Walter Schmidt."

"It's my gas now, Mrs. Baumgartner. I'm buying your car."

"All right, but don't you let that boy of yours drive it."

"Norm's only twelve," Dad said. "He can't drive."

"That didn't stop him when he was . . . what? . . . about five or six. He drove a truck right through the front window of the store, Sam. You should've seen it. Knocked down a whole display of grapefruits."

"It wasn't through the window. I just bumped the back of the store a little."

"Don't you tell me what I saw with my own eyes. Glass and grapefruits flying. Little children screaming for their mothers. It was absolutely terrifying."

I wasn't going to argue with her. Carl and even Leon knew enough not to laugh. We waited at the end of the driveway while Sam and Dad finished the deal. Sam siphoned a little gas from his own car to make sure we'd have enough to get home. Then we climbed in and took off in our brand-new old-lady's car.

From then on, every time Mrs. Baumgartner came into the store, she'd ask me if I had driven her car. Then she'd describe the truck incident to anyone who would listen. The way she told it, you'd have thought I crashed the Hindenburg into our produce section. Oh, and then she'd always ask me if my hand had started growing back yet.

Chapter 20

*M*om, I can't go to school today," I said. "I don't feel good."

Mom looked up from the breakfast table. "That couldn't have anything to do with the fact that today is the fifteenth of April, could it?"

"What's so special about April 15? Is it somebody's birthday?"

Mom shook her head. "You really thought you could pull the wool over my eyes, Norm?"

"Aw, Mom, please let me stay home. I can't miss the Giants' opening game. It's not fair that they start playing on a school day."

"I know, but you can't miss school. I'll listen to the game in the store, so I can tell you about it. If it goes into extra innings, you might get home in time to hear the end of it."

I knew there wasn't much chance of that. Our bus went all over creation before it got to our house. We never made it in less than an hour. All I could think of that day was the game. But then the only thing that could take my mind off the Giants happened.

We got to play baseball in gym for the first time since fall.

This time Mr. Locke had us count off so the odd numbers were on one team and the evens on the other. When we saw what was happening, Leon and I put one person between us so we'd be on the same team. "I got a new right-handed glove for you, Norm," Mr. Locke said. "You're playing right field."

"Thanks, sir, that's great."

Leon was center field. As we walked out he came over to me. "You won't get many balls out there, but if one comes your way, I'll back you up."

"I've been practicing," I said. "I can do this. Stay in center."

"Okay." Leon shrugged, but he looked worried.

The glove wasn't broken in at all. I shoved my hand into it and leaned over as if I was catching a grounder, then pulled the glove off with my elbow and pretended to take the ball out and throw it. It was hard to get my hand back into the glove because it was so stiff. I took the glove off again and tried to bend it back and forth against my chest to make it open up more. But then I heard Mr. Locke yell, "Play ball!" so I had to start paying attention.

Carl was the third one up to bat on his team. Poor kid struck out. I could see that he started swinging too late. I'd have to remember to tell him that. Nothing came my way for the whole first inning. When Leon and I were sitting by the fence, waiting for our turns at bat, I was still working at breaking in the glove.

"Give it here," Leon said, grabbing it out of my hand. "This thing is like cement. If Mr. Locke will let me take it home tonight, I'll oil it for you."

"I thought you didn't want me playing baseball."

"What am I, your keeper? If you're gonna play, I can't stop you, so I might as well try to keep you from making a fool of yourself."

"Gee, thanks for the vote of confidence."

"You're not welcome."

Leon was up to bat right before me. He hit a grounder down the first base line and was out on the first pitch.

As I passed him on the way to bat, I said, "Speaking of making a fool of yourself . . ."

Leon didn't look at me, but he couldn't help smiling.

Mr. Locke was surprised when I took the left-handed batting position. "You're on the wrong side, Norm," he whispered, as if he thought I had lost my brain along with my hand.

"It works better for me this way," I said. "I've been practicing." The pitcher wound up and let loose. I was so used to having the ball zing back to me from a short distance on the rope that this ball seemed like it was coming at me in slow motion. I had plenty of time to size it up and aim my swing. I connected with the ball and hit it high out into right field.

As I ran for first, I heard Leon yelling for me to keep going, so I rounded second and slid into third just before Charlie Ackerman could tag me. I couldn't believe it! A triple on my first at-bat! Kids were cheering for me—even Carl in the outfield and some of the guys on his team. Leon had two fingers in his mouth, and he was whistling through his teeth.

When I crossed home plate on Ronnie Cressman's double, Mr. Locke reached out to shake my hand. "Nice going, Norm. You've improved a lot."

"I've been working at it," I said. All the kids were slapping me on the back as I went by them.

When our side took the field again, Leon tossed me the glove. "It's still stiff, but not as bad as before."

"Thanks."

I practiced getting the glove on and off a few times and it worked better. It was partway through the inning with a runner on first when Gordie Corrigan came up to bat. He took the left-handed batting position.

"What's he doing?" I said to Leon. "Doesn't he bat right-handed?"

"He's a strong batter on either side." Leon started moving to the right. "He's going to slam one out into right field. Wants to make you look bad."

"I'm okay," I said. "I can handle it."

It wasn't until the third pitch that Gordie hit a hard ground ball between first and second. I got down on one knee so the ball wouldn't get past me. I scooped it up in my glove, slipped the glove off, and threw the ball to second. It worked smooth as frozen custard, but I was too late. The runner on first had rounded second and made it to third. I was sure a two-handed player could have made the out. Just the couple of seconds it took to get that glove off made me miss it. Still, I hadn't fumbled the ball. I just needed to speed up.

Once gym class was over, I couldn't wait for the

bus to get me home. I ran into the store. Mom was making potato salad in the back room. "Hey, Mom, is the game still going?"

"Just ended about fifteen minutes ago."

"Did the Giants win?"

She scooped the salad into a deli tray. "Nope."

"They lost to the Phillies?"

"I'm afraid so."

"I'm glad I missed it, then. I hate when they lose. Hey, guess what, though, Mom?"

"What?"

"We played baseball in gym and I got a triple."

Mom looked up and smiled. "That's wonderful, Norm. All that practicing in the back yard is paying off."

"You've been watching me?"

She came around the counter. "Let's just say mothers are like Santa Claus. They see you when you're sleeping, they know when you're . . ."

"Aw, Mom. You know I hate that song."

The same thing happened again on Thursday. I played pretty well in gym, but the Giants lost a second game to the Phillies. I didn't get another triple, but I got on base twice. I was still having trouble in the field, though. No matter how hard I tried, I just wasn't fast enough. I was worried about the Giants, too. They were playing the Dodgers on the weekend. They couldn't lose to their worst rivals.

I got up early on Saturday to sort the Sunday newspapers. We sold five different New York papers. The special sections were delivered to us starting on Thursday. We stored them under the newspaper table at the front of the store. On Saturday I had to put all the sections together so they were ready to slip into the papers when they were dropped off Sunday morning. The *Journal American*s were easy because we got only about fifteen of them, but we had about a hundred copies of the *Daily News* and maybe thirty-five *New York Times,* so they took a lot longer.

I pulled off the leftover Friday editions and started to put them under the table with the week's papers that would be sent back Monday morning. Then I spotted a Giants story in the sports section of the *Daily Mirror* and settled down to read. It said the Phillies won the two games with the Giants because of their outfielders—especially the center fielder, who rushed the grounders and line drives and saved himself several seconds by meeting the ball halfway instead of waiting for it to get to him. That was the answer to my fielding problem. I might not be able to get any faster handling the glove, but I could run forward to meet the ball and shave off time that way. I couldn't wait to try it.

"Norman," Dad called from the back of the store. "You're supposed to be working, not reading. Customers will be coming in any minute. Get those papers straightened out."

"Okay, Dad." I quickly finished sorting and went out back to practice fielding. It was hard to get the ball to do what I wanted it to by bouncing it off the wall, but I was doing the best I could.

"Want me to hit some to you?" It was Leon.

"Sure. Let's move out into the field where there's more room."

I didn't ask what caused Leon's change of heart. I was just glad to have his help. Each time he hit a ball to me, I'd start charging. When I was about halfway to the ball, I'd drop to one knee and scoop it up with my glove.

"Charge it even more," Leon said. "You're still waiting for it to get to you."

"I don't want the ball to get past me."

"It won't. Just push it a few more steps."

He was right. I could run until the ball was almost at my feet and still get it.

We had been practicing about half an hour when Carl showed up. He had been coming around quite a bit lately. "You guys playing baseball?"

"Nah," Leon said. "It's a new kind of badminton you play with a bat."

Carl just stood there shading his eyes from the sun.

"Why can't we let him play just this once?" I whispered to Leon.

Leon rolled his eyes at me, then turned to Carl. "So are you gonna make like a statue or play ball?"

Carl's face brightened up. "Sure, I'll play. I don't have a glove or bat or anything, though."

"You can use my old left-handed glove in the garage," I said.

We practiced for the rest of the morning until it was time to listen to the Giants–Dodgers game. The Giants won. Leon, Carl, Mom, and I ate a whole carton of Neapolitan ice cream to celebrate after the game.

Chapter 21

After that day, Carl just happened to show up more and more when Leon and I were practicing. Sometimes he played, and other times he watched. I figured we were just about his only friends. Besides no kid wants to stay home with his grandmother all the time, even if she does bake great stuff.

Leon didn't seem to mind having him hang around. It didn't matter that Carl was a lousy player and didn't care that much about baseball. Now with the three of us, we could take turns at batting, fielding, and the thing I really wanted to do—pitching. I had been getting pretty good at hitting the rectangle I had drawn on the wall, but pitching to a real person was different. For one thing, the batter moved around, taking swings between pitches, and that threw me off. At first even Carl got a few hits off me, but I started to get better, until I could strike out Leon once in a while.

One day at the end of gym class, Mr. Locke held up a sheet of paper. "This is the signup sheet for the summer baseball league. It's for ages eleven through thirteen. If you're interested in joining, put your name on the list. I'll be needing about sixteen players plus a couple of alternates."

Charlie Ackerman raised his hand. "What if too many guys sign up? Will you have tryouts to decide who makes the team?"

Mr. Locke shook his head. "You've been trying out since the first gym class this year. I know how all of you play, so I'll make my decision based on what I've seen. Look for the list on the last day of school."

Leon and I got in line to sign up, and Carl waited with us. "This isn't fair," I said. "I thought we'd have time to get ready for a tryout. If he counts how we've been all along in gym, I'm out for sure."

"Improvement has to count for something," Carl said. "You're a lot better than you were last fall."

Leon snorted. "That's the understatement of the year. You were awful."

"Gee, thanks for pointing that out, Leon. I'm worried enough about making the team. If Mr. Locke is only picking eighteen players out of all the sixth, seventh, and eighth grades, we're up against at least a hundred kids."

"I think it's more like seventy-five," Carl said.

"And half of them are girls, so we're only talking about . . ." Leon was thinking, trying to divide in his head, which was useless because he couldn't even do it with a paper and pencil.

"Thirty-seven or thirty-eight," Carl said, "but some kids won't want to play, and some will be going away on vacation, so that might knock out another ten."

Carl went to the end of the line so he could check

how many signed up. Meanwhile, Mr. Locke let loose with one more bombshell. "Even though the summer league isn't connected with school, I have my own rule for my team. If you have even one D on your final report card, you can't play."

"Only one D?" Leon whispered. "For me, that's a really good report card."

Last year I could have said the same thing, but Mom and Miss Bean had been pestering me so much about homework this year, I wasn't getting anything lower than a C. I was shaky in spelling, so I'd have to study harder. It would be stupid to play well enough to make the team and then fail because of my grades.

We waited for Carl. "Thirty-one kids signed up," he said. "So thirteen will be cut. Of course, some might be knocked out because of grades."

Leon's shoulders slumped. "Yeah, like me."

"Or me," I added to make him feel better.

"Too bad we're not brains like Carl," Leon said. "He could make the team easy with his grades. Of course, there's the small point that he can't play. Good thing you don't want to be in the league, Carl."

"But I do," Carl said. "I signed up."

"Why?" I asked. "You don't even like sports."

Carl shrugged. "I like practicing with you guys. Maybe I'll get better at it."

Leon shook his head. "Wait a minute. Why should we help you with baseball so you could get on the team and take away a spot from Norm or me?"

"Because I could help you get your grades up, that's why."

Leon looked at me. "He has a point."

So that's when we launched into Operation Summer League. We decided to do our homework together every day after school, then practice baseball after supper until dark. The best part of the plan was that we needed only one set of books for all of us. This was a big relief, since Miss Bean was really piling on the homework to fit everything in by the end of the year. One day last week I had to carry five textbooks.

That afternoon, we were doing arithmetic in our kitchen when Mom came up from the store. "Norm, you'll have to play with your friends later. We got in a big order and it needs to be shelved." She turned to go back down the stairs.

"But, Mom," I said, "we're doing homework."

"I don't care what you're doing. I need to have you—" She stuck her head back into the kitchen. "You're doing what?"

"We can't have any Ds if we want to play in the summer baseball league, Mrs. Schmidt," Leon said. "Carl's a brain, so he's helping us."

"Then you all could use some brain food." Mom put a package of Fig Newtons on the table. "Where's Ellie? She can start helping out in the store."

"I think she's across the street at Ginny's, Mom." I felt a little guilty for telling on her, but it was about time Ellie started pulling her weight around here.

That night at dinner, I told Mom and Dad about our plan to make the team. "Coach Locke takes sixth-, seventh-, and eighth-graders, so we'll have to be extra good to make it. He's going to cut thirteen kids."

"I'm glad to see you all working so hard on the schoolwork," Mom said. "You're excused from being in the store on school days."

Ellie looked miserable. "It's not fair. Norm gets to play baseball and I have to work in the store."

"We were going to have you start working when school was out, so you're just beginning a month early," Mom said. "Besides, Norm is getting excused to do homework, not play baseball."

"Don't get your heart set on making the team," Dad said. "Some kids will have to be disappointed." He got up and left. I wanted to call out, "Thanks for the encouragement, Dad." I sure wished he would come around the way Leon had.

The next month was a blur of school, homework, and baseball. We watched how the other guys played in gym to guess who would make the team.

"Charlie Ackerman is a good infielder," I said. "And Ronnie Cressman is a power hitter even though he's not that fast at running the bases."

"Ronnie's like Babe Ruth," Leon said. "He makes enough homers so he doesn't have to worry about being able to run."

One day I asked Mr. Locke to let me try pitching. He did, and I really flubbed it. The first batter up against me was Gordie, and my pitches went wild—four balls in a row. Gordie mouthed the word "cripple" as he walked to first. I wished I had beaned him on the noggin with one of those balls.

I was practicing by myself Saturday morning when Ellie came out. "Norm, would you do me a favor?"

She had been mad about having to work in the store, and I felt a little guilty about that, since she was doing some of my chores.

"Maybe. What kind of favor?"

"Teach me how to hit. The boys in gym make fun of how the girls bat."

It was a good thing Leon wasn't there, because he didn't think girls had any business playing baseball in gym or anywhere else.

I gave Ellie the bat. "Okay, let's see what you can do."

She took a couple of practice swings.

"Well, first of all, you're standing like a girl."

"I *am* a girl."

"Not if you want to bat like a boy, you're not. Girls always stand with their knees straight and their rear ends sticking out."

Ellie looked over her shoulder. "My rear end is not sticking out!"

"You going to argue or learn? Bend your knees and keep them loose."

Ellie bent her knees.

"That's better. Here comes the pitch."

She swung, missed, and kept spinning around.

"That's ballet, not baseball."

"I can't help it if I'm graceful."

"Keep your feet planted in one place. Don't take your eye off the ball."

We worked at it for about half an hour, and Ellie hit one every now and then. "You're doing better," I said, "but we should stop. Mom will be calling us in for lunch any minute now."

"Just a few more, Normie. Please? I want to really clobber one."

I threw her a hard pitch. She swung and hit a high fly ball. Then I heard glass breaking behind my back. "Holy cow! It's the dining-room window. Run!"

I don't know why I thought it would do any good to run, as if Mom wouldn't figure out who was playing baseball in our back yard. She opened the kitchen window as we were taking off. "You kids get back here!"

We hid behind the Happy Valley for a while, then I decided Mom would be harder on us if we stayed away than if we went back and faced the music. Besides, she always went easy on Ellie.

When we got upstairs, Mom blamed me for breaking the window. I looked at Ellie. She didn't say a word. A guy couldn't squeal on a girl even if she was his bratty kid sister, so I let her get away with it. Then, in the middle of lunch, when Mom was still letting me have it, Ellie spoke up. "Norm didn't hit that ball. I did."

"You expect me to believe that you hit that ball hard enough to break a second-floor window," Mom said.

Ellie nodded. She looked real pleased with herself.

The last day of school finally arrived. We had an assembly where each teacher called her class to the stage to get their report cards. A lot of parents came to see their kids move up to the next grade—mostly mothers, because the fathers worked. Mom took off from the store so she could come see Ellie and me.

Miss Bean handed me my report card. "Nice work, Norm. I knew you could do it." I sneaked a look on the way back to my seat. I had a C, three Bs, and my first-ever A. I couldn't wait to show that to Mom.

At the end of the assembly, the seniors stood on the stage and sang the Carmel Alma Mater and the Senior Farewell. After the singing, we all went to the gym for punch and cookies.

"Get a load of this, guys." Leon waved his report card. "All C minuses."

"That's good," Carl said.

Leon's eyes got wide. "Good? Come on, Carl, it's a miracle!"

"That's the understatement of the year," I said, and we all laughed.

Carl looked at me. "How about you, Norm?"

I slipped my report card into my back pocket. "Same here. No Ds."

"Hey, Norm," Leon said. "Why is your mother talking with Mr. Locke?"

I looked over my shoulder. Sure enough, there were Mom and Mr. Locke having a serious discussion. "Oh, no! I have to stop her! She's probably telling him not to put me on the team."

"Why would she do that?" Carl asked.

"She wants me to work hard for everything."

"You have worked hard," Leon said. "She knows that."

"You don't understand. She doesn't want me selling pencils."

Carl was puzzled. "Do we have to sell pencils for scouts? Like the Girl Scouts sell cookies?"

"No! Selling pencils as a job!"

I ran over to where Mom and Mr. Locke were talking. "Mr. Locke, please don't listen to my mother."

Mr. Locke looked surprised. "You being modest, Norm?"

"What?"

"Your mother was just telling me about how hard you've been practicing. She didn't have to tell me that, though."

"She didn't?"

"No. I could see that by how much you've improved. You and Leon have helped Carl Oberndorfer, too, I hear."

"Yeah, well, he helped us get our grades up."

"Sounds like you guys are good friends."

I nodded, not sure where this conversation was going.

"You'll all have a good time playing on my team this summer, then."

"All of us made the team?"

"You sure did. You're hard workers. I like that." He held out the list. He had Carl and me as outfielders, and Leon on second base.

"Thanks, Mr. Locke! I gotta go tell them."

Later, as Mom and I were walking to the car, I asked her, "How come you didn't tell Mr. Locke to be hard on me like you did with my other teachers?"

"After you told us about the summer league, I did go in to see him. I said I didn't want him to put you on the team just because you lost the hand, if that's what you mean. I told him you should earn your spot like any other boy."

"Mom! Why would you say a thing like that?"

"Would you want to make the team because the coach felt sorry for you?"

"Well, sure, if that's the only way I could get on it."

"I know you don't mean that. And you didn't need sympathy to make the team, did you? You made it by working hard. You know what your coach said about you?"

"What?"

"He told me he had never seen anyone improve as fast as you. He said you're a strong player and you have a lot of heart." I thought I saw tears in her eyes just before she gave me a hug. "I'm really proud of you, Norm."

I had to admit I was pretty proud of myself.

Chapter 22

*B*aseball practice started the next week, every Monday, Wednesday, and Thursday from ten to twelve at the school baseball field. Our games were scheduled for Tuesdays and Thursdays at six. We had been right about the other kids in our class to make the team—Charlie Ackerman, Ronnie Cressman, and Gordie Corrigan. There were six kids from seventh grade and six from eighth. Mr. Locke explained that he had divided the team equally among the three grades. "This way you younger guys will have three years to learn and get better before you move up to the older league. Some of the coaches from the other towns are just out for the win, so you'll be up against teams with mostly eighth-graders. But remember it's skill that counts, not size. This is Mr. Hagen, the high school social studies teacher. He'll be your assistant coach. Enough talking. Let's get started."

I had thought we would divide into two teams and play a game, but it wasn't like that. One of the older kids was assigned to hit balls for some of us to field, while Coach Hagen pitched for batting practice and

Coach Locke worked with kids on running bases and sliding. Then we'd switch groups so everybody got practice on everything.

We didn't get to practice pitching, though. The pitchers were both eighth-graders, and they practiced with the two catchers. I knew one of the catchers, Eddie Shapiro. He came into our store a lot. He was an eighth-grader.

Starting the first day, I asked Coach Hagen if I could pitch for batting practice. "Not today. . . . What's your name?"

"Norm."

"Right. Norm. You need to be practicing the skills you need for the games. Maybe another day."

I asked him every day, but his answer was always the same. I still practiced pitching at the strike zone I had drawn on the wall at home, so when I got the chance to prove myself, I'd be ready.

Halfway through June, we had our first game. Coach Locke brought a big carton filled with old Carmel High School baseball uniforms. "These aren't new, but they'll make us look like a team when we take the field. Try to find a uniform that fits you."

The older guys dug in right away to claim their uniforms from last year. By the time we got to the carton, there wasn't much left. "These things are all ripped up," Leon said. "Where did they come from, anyway?"

Eddie Shapiro laughed. "Every time the high school gets new uniforms, Coach grabs the ones they're throwing away. I bet some of these go back to the thirties. Besides, the guys from the older league get first dibs, so we get the leftovers." He pulled out a shirt and handed it to me. "This should fit you, Norm."

"Thanks, Eddie."

The shirts had probably been blue and white when they were new, but now they were blue and gray. Still, when I put mine on, I felt like a million bucks.

Coach Hagen lined us up. "Let's check the numbers. Since these uniforms are from all different years, sometimes we have duplicates."

I looked over at Ronnie Cressman. He had a letter missing, so his shirt said CAR EL. Another guy had CARM.

"Looks like we have two number sevens."

One was me and the other was an older kid. "I've always had seven, Coach," he said. "It's my lucky number."

"You have seniority, Bill. It looks like you'll have to find another shirt, Norm."

I went back to the carton. It was mostly pants in there now. There were a couple of shirts big enough to fit an ox, and another with a rip all the way down the back. Way at the bottom, I found the only other shirt. I couldn't believe my luck. It looked about my size. I put it on and ran back to the group.

I heard Gordie snort as I walked by him. "Get a load of what it says on Norm's shirt."

I looked down. My shirt had so many letters missing, it spelled ARM.

Gordie followed me. "That's the perfect shirt for the team cripple. They got you labeled, Norm."

I turned around and held my stump in front of his nose. "You think I need a sign on my shirt to make people notice this?"

"I like that shirt." Leon had moved in beside me. "Norm the Arm. Sounds like a power pitcher."

Coach Locke came over. "Is there a problem here, boys?"

"There's no problem, Coach," I said. "No problem at all."

Our first game was against Patterson on the Carmel field. Mom was there, but Dad said he had to wait until the store closed. We won 8–2.

I played my best game ever. I scored two runs out of three times on base, threw a Patterson runner out on second, and caught a fly ball for the last out. After the game I noticed this guy was going around talking to some of our players. He looked kind of familiar, so I asked Eddie Shapiro who he was.

"That's the high school baseball coach. He comes to the summer league to see what kind of players are coming up."

I could see the coach talking with Ronnie Cressman. Then he walked over to us and shook Eddie's hand. "You're turning into a fine catcher, Eddie. You made some good plays tonight."

"Thanks, Coach."

I stood there smiling at the coach. I knew I had played well, and I was waiting for him to say something. The guy barely looked at me, then walked over to some other kids, without saying a word. I wondered if it was because of the hand. Maybe he wouldn't even consider me for the team when I got to high school. I'd show him. I'd get so good, he'd have to ask me to play.

We played Mahopac and Pawling in the next couple of weeks and beat both of them. I was getting better at batting and fielding, but I could see that I would never get to pitch because the two eighth-graders, George Kaiser and Dirk Swenson, had the pitcher's spot locked up. Still, I kept trying to pitch for batting practice, until one day, it paid off. It was my turn up at bat when Coach Hagen was called over to the side of the field to talk to someone. "Norm," he said. "Put down the bat and pitch for me, will you?"

"Sure, Coach!" I couldn't believe I was getting a chance at last.

Bill Kravitz, one of the older kids, was up next. I wound up and threw one on the top outside corner and he swung at it but missed. He swung and missed the next one, too.

"Come on," Bill said. "This is batting practice, not a game. You're supposed to be throwing lollipops so we can hit them."

Eddie Shapiro was catching. "You should be able to hit good pitches, Bill. Keep it up, Norm."

The rule was that each batter got to make five hits before his turn was up. Nobody had ever said how many strikes they could have. Since Bill seemed to have trouble with the high outsiders, that's what I kept throwing. He missed the next three. "This is a waste of time. Have somebody pitch who knows what he's doing."

"Nothing's wrong with Norm's pitching," Eddie said. "He's throwing strikes."

"He is not!" Bill threw down the bat and walked off.

"Okay, new rule," Eddie said. "Everybody just gets ten hittable pitches. Whether you connect or not is your problem."

Ronnie Cressman was up next. He usually crunched the ball way out in the outfield. I gave him a pitch that was just inside the strike zone. It threw him off balance, and his hit dribbled only to the infield. My next four pitches were to the upper and lower inside corners of the strike box. I could almost see my chalk drawing on the wall as I pitched. Ronnie hit all of them, but not one got farther than the infield. At the end of his turn, Ronnie gave me a thumbs-up as he handed the bat to Jim Sykes, our strongest hitter.

I had watched Jim bat a lot, because I wanted to know what made him so good. When a ball came in high, he swung at it every time, but missed. He was best at hitting low and outside. So I pitched him five balls that just skimmed the top inside corner of the strike zone. He whiffed every one of them.

By now, Bill had brought Coach Hagen back to the batting practice. "See?" Bill said. "All the kid is throwing is balls. He couldn't hit the strike zone with a bowling ball."

"Is that how you see it, Eddie?" Coach Hagen asked.

"They look like strikes to me," Eddie said. "He's got a lot of control. Lobs them in right on the corners."

Just then, Coach Locke blew a whistle to call us together. "Our next game is at Brewster on Friday night. Brewster is a big school with lights on the field, so the game doesn't start until seven-thirty. Remember that Friday is the Fourth of July. If you go to a picnic or parade that day, you need to be back here six o'clock sharp to get a ride to the game. If you're late, we leave without you. Brewster is our toughest team, so we'll need plenty of warm-up."

I could hardly sleep the night before the game. It was a whole year since I lost my hand. No matter how hard I tried, I couldn't stop thinking about that. I was supposed to go to New York pretty soon to get my hook. I wasn't so sure I wanted one, now that I'd learned how to do just about everything without it. If I couldn't use it to bat, catch, or throw, what good was it? And what if I accidentally hit somebody with it when I was sliding into base? When I finally got to sleep, I had a creepy dream about trying to play baseball with a meat hook fastened to the end of my stump.

The Brewster team looked tough the minute they came out on the field.

"There's nobody younger than eighth grade on that team," I said.

"Are you kidding?" Leon said. "If those are eighth-graders, they've been left back a year or two. Their pitcher is growing a mustache, for Pete's sake."

"Don't let their size intimidate you," Coach Locke

said. "Baseball is a game of brains, not brawn. If you play smart, you can win."

Not even the older guys on our team looked like they believed that.

Brewster clobbered us right from the beginning. Their guys were really strong hitters. Coach Locke started with George Kaiser, our second strongest pitcher. He was saving Dirk Swenson for when things got bad. When Coach read the list of starters, Carl, Leon, Ronnie, and I were assigned to the bench.

"Big deal that Coach picks kids from all the grades," Leon said. "If he doesn't play younger kids in tough games, he shouldn't put us on the team."

The Brewster guys were slamming balls all over the outfield. Gordie was in my spot, and he and the other outfielders were hustling. If I had to sit out a game, this was the one to miss.

I wanted to study the Brewster batters, but I couldn't see well enough from the bench. I wandered over to the wire backstop so I was in a position right behind the catcher. Nobody paid any attention to me. Maybe I wasn't good enough to be played in a hard-hitting game, but the least I could do was learn something. I was glad Mom and Dad weren't here to see me sitting out the game, though. Mom hadn't been able to leave the store early, but she said she and Dad would try to get here by the time the game started. I should've known they wouldn't make it.

By the end of the second inning, George Kaiser had given up six hits. That's when Coach put in our big gun, Dirk Swenson. Quite a few Carmel parents had come to the game. The worse we got, the louder they cheered for us. There were about twice as many fans from Brewster. They were even louder, screaming and whistling every time their team scored.

Watching the Brewster guys bat, I saw that number eight missed two low inside pitches. Then Dirk delivered one down the middle and the kid clobbered it for a triple. Number ten would swing at anything high in the strike zone, but he couldn't hit them. When he had two strikes, I was hoping Dirk would send in another high one, but instead he put it in the center and the kid smashed it way out into left field. The crack of his bat was like gunfire. Number fourteen couldn't hit anything that came near his hands, but he'd reach for outside balls and launch them like a rocket.

Coach put Leon into the game, so I went back to the bench in case he wanted me, too. Fat chance!

By the bottom of the fifth inning, the score was 10–0. The Brewster guys were getting real cocky now. As one of them rounded third, heading for a home run, he yelled, "Hey, you Carmel Corn Candy Apples, this game is over in the next inning. This is easier than batting practice."

"How could the game be over in the next inning?" Carl asked. "Don't we have four more at bats?"

"If one team gets fourteen runs over the other, they call the game," Ronnie said. "They figure no team can come from that far behind. The way we're going, Brewster can get four runs in the next inning easy."

Carmel still didn't score any runs in the top of the sixth. Before we took the field, Coach Locke called us together. "All right, boys, you put up a good fight. I told you Brewster is a tough team. Just do your best until the game is over. And, Norm, I'm putting you in as pitcher."

My stomach dropped to my feet. "Me? Against them?"

"It's what you've been asking for, isn't it? This is your chance to show what you've got. Coach Hagen said you did a good job pitching for batting practice the other day."

"I know, but that was . . ."

"No buts, Norm. Get out there and pitch."

Gordie had just heard what was happening. "The cripple is pitching?"

Coach Locke pointed to him. "Corrigan, I've given you the benefit of the doubt since the beginning of the school year, but I don't like your attitude. As of right now, you're out of the game. Go sit on the far end of the bench. I'll deal with you later."

My head was spinning too much to enjoy the fact that Gordie had just been benched. Eddie Shapiro took me over to home plate. "Don't worry, Norm. I'll give you signals. This means fast ball." He slipped two fingers down into his mitt.

"I don't have a fast ball."

"Okay, this is a change-up."

"What does that mean?"

"An off-speed ball. It's slower than your . . . never mind. This is for a curve ball. You have a curve ball?"

"No." I felt miserable. How could I be a pitcher? I didn't know anything.

Eddie put his hand on my shoulder. "We'll skip the signals. Just do what you did at batting practice. You were fine."

"But I can't pull us out of this mess."

"Are you kidding? Nobody could pull us out of this mess. Everybody knows that. The coach is giving you a chance to try out your pitching arm, you know? It's not going to make any difference one way or the other."

Just as the umpire called "Carmel take the field," the sun dipped below the trees and the lights went on.

As I walked out to the pitcher's mound, I felt like I was going to my own hanging with a spotlight on me. Worse yet, everybody knew Coach was only letting me pitch because Carmel had already lost. Some of the Brewster fans got up and started to leave. I heard one guy say, "This thing is over. They're putting in a little kid as pitcher."

"Look," someone said. "The poor kid only has one hand."

When I turned around, I saw the Brewster guys on the bench, pointing at me, elbowing each other, and laughing.

Okay, now I was mad. Maybe I didn't have a chance of pulling this game out, but Coach was right. I'd been begging to pitch and this was my chance. I wasn't going to flub it.

I wound up and threw my first practice pitch. It was way out of the strike zone. Eddie gave me a hand signal I understood. It meant slow down and take it easy. This time I imagined the chalk rectangle and sent one right into the middle. Eddie gave me the thumbs-up and threw the ball back to me. I was so fast with getting the glove on and off now, I didn't even think about it. I took a dozen more pitches, aiming for the corners of the strike zone. Finally the umpire came over. "Okay, kid, you have to get going here."

The first Brewster batter came up. It was number fourteen. Right away I saw that he was the one who crowded the plate, so I sent him insiders. He jumped back with one, saying that I was trying to hit him.

"That was a good pitch," the umpire said.

After two strikes, I did get one ball called against me, but then fourteen swung at another insider and missed. I had struck out my first player! The people on the Carmel bleachers went nuts cheering.

Next came the guy with the mustache. He got a single off me. I remembered something from watching him in the earlier innings, so I called over Bill, our first baseman, to talk.

I slipped him the ball. "This guy likes to wander off first base, so pretend I have the ball. You go back and tag him when he steps off the bag."

"Okay, but remember you can't be on the mound without the ball."

"I know."

Bill went back to first, hiding the ball in his glove. I walked back toward the mound, then stopped, pretending to be fixing something on my glove. It was quiet now. I heard somebody from Brewster say, "Come on. Let's get this thing over with."

Then the umpire yelled, "Runner out on first!"

I turned around, and Bill grinned as he threw me the ball. We did it!

I gave up two more hits. Now we had runners on first and second. I had to get the next batter out— number seventeen. I couldn't remember anything about him, so I tried sending one to the upper outside corner. He didn't swing.

"Strike one!"

I did the same thing again.

"Strike two!"

I figured he'd swing at the next one, so I pitched it low and outside. He swung at it.

"Strike three!"

When we came back to the bench, Coach Locke pounded me on the back. "That's what I mean about playing smart. Did you guys see that play that Bill and Norm pulled off on first? Have you been watching the control Norm is using when he pitches? I want you all to get smart when you bat. You're trying to clobber the ball for a home run. You don't have enough control and your swings are going wild. Slow down and connect with the ball so we get some base runners."

I was up to bat for the first time in this game. All the Brewster players moved in. I swung at the first pitch and missed. They moved in more because they figured I didn't have the strength to send it past the infield. I hit the next pitch between the shortstop and third baseman. I made it to first as the ball rolled out into left field. "Cheap hit," the first baseman said. He was right. If they had been playing their positions, the shortstop would have caught the ball and sent it to first for the out. After that, a couple of our guys got singles, which put me on third. Then Ronnie hit a high fly. As soon as the ball was caught, I took off for home. I slid in just before the ball. I had scored the first run for Carmel!

More Carmel players were connecting with the ball now. The other team made some errors, so our guys got on base and drove in some runs. We scored three more runs in the top of the seventh, making it 10–4.

My next time on the mound, I had more confidence. If I took my time, I could put the ball where I wanted it. Some of the Brewster runners were calling me names like Lefty and Loser, but I didn't let them rattle me. Between my pitching and some good plays in the field, Brewster didn't score in the seventh.

We managed to get three guys on base in the eighth, then Jim Sykes hit a homer, driving in four runs. Now we were cooking with gas! It was 10–8. Was there a chance we could win this thing?

It was the bottom of the eighth with one out, and I was getting tired. I had let a couple of guys on base by losing concentration. To kill a little time, I looked over my shoulder. Carl was playing way too deep in center field. I motioned for him to move in, but he shook his head. I wasn't going to argue with him, so I turned around and pitched. The batter slammed a long fly.

Carl must have known this guy was a power hitter. Why hadn't I remembered that? This was a homer for sure. Now Brewster would get three more runs, making it 13–8. We couldn't possibly score five runs in our last at bat.

Suddenly there was a burst of cheering from the Carmel bleachers. I turned around and saw Carl firing the ball to second to put out a runner. As we ran back to the bench, everybody was clapping Carl on the back.

"You should have seen him, Norm," Leon said. "The ball is coming out way over his head and Carl keeps going back and back and he reaches up and catches it."

"I just put my hand up to keep from falling over," Carl said. "The ball dropped into my glove."

By the top of the ninth, Brewster was out for blood. Brewster's second baseman practically tackled Charlie to get him out. Then, with two outs, Ronnie hit a homer. We got only one run out of it because nobody was on base, but the Carmel crowd went wild. Now it was 10–9, only one down. Both sides were cheering for their teams.

Jim Sykes was up next, and I was on deck. This was the most exciting moment of my life. Jim always got a hit. He might slam a homer for the tying run. Then it was up to me to get on base. Maybe I could even make the winning run. But what if I messed up? I wiped the sweat out of my eyes. I couldn't think about that. I had to concentrate. I kept taking practice swings with an extra bat. I had to get a hit.

When Jim stepped up to the plate, the people in the bleachers got real quiet. Everybody knew he was a power hitter. He swung on the first pitch and hit a line drive to left field. The Brewster fielder made a tumbling catch for the third out. Suddenly it was all over!

I felt like I'd been standing on a trap door that opened and dropped me into a pit. The Brewster crowd went nuts. After we lined up on the field to shake hands with the Brewster players, Coach Locke called our team together. "You guys should be proud of yourselves. You played a great game."

"But we lost," I said.

Coach shook his head. "It's not all about the final score. It's about playing smart. Tonight you all showed yourselves that if you don't give up, you can do amazing things. That's an important thing to remember for life, not just baseball. Now everybody get rested and we'll see you at practice on Monday."

The other kids started off looking for their families. Coach Locke called me over.

"Norm, I know you were disappointed about losing, but from the time you got into the game, you beat Brewster 9–0. I bet you didn't think about that, did you?"

"No, sir."

"I want you to start working out with the other pitchers. You've got a lot of control, but we need to add more pitches to your repertoire."

"Yes, sir!"

"Go find your family. They'll want to congratulate you on your game."

"They couldn't make it, Coach."

"I'm sure I saw your mother." He looked around. "There she is."

Mom and Ellie were coming toward me, and right behind them was Dad. Ellie ran up and gave me a hug. "I'm going to tell everybody my brother is the pitcher for the Carmel team."

"One of the pitchers," I corrected.

Mom put her hands on my cheeks. "I always knew you could do anything you put your mind to. From now on, the sky's the limit, Norm."

That sounded like Mom wouldn't be letting up on me any time soon.

Just then Leon came running over. "Mr. and Mrs. Schmidt, they're having fireworks. Can Norm stay and watch them with me? My dad can drive him home."

"We'll all stay," Dad said. "I'll walk Norm over to the car to put away his gear. He'll meet you in the bleachers."

"The top row," Leon said. "That's the best view. I'll save you a seat, Norm."

Dad started toward the parking lot. I was going to tell him I could just hang on to my glove instead of putting it in the car, but I could tell he wanted to talk about something.

On the way to the car, Dad stopped in front of a turquoise '47 Studebaker. "That's a good-looking car."

"Sure is."

"It reminds me of the ones you draw. Not so pointy on the fenders, though."

"No, but it looks like it's leaning forward, doesn't it? Like it can't wait for somebody to step on its gas pedal."

Dad laughed. "That's a good one, Norm. A car that's raring to go." Dad got quiet again as we kept walking. Then he said, "That was some game."

"Yeah, it was."

"If you had told me one year ago that I'd be watching my son pitch like you did tonight . . ." His voice cracked. "I was afraid you'd never be able . . . and now look at you."

We walked along in silence a couple more minutes until we reached our car. Dad opened the door. I tossed my glove on the back seat.

"Yes, sir. That was some pitching job you did."

"Thanks, Dad."

As we walked back to the baseball field, Dad reached over and patted my back a couple of times. I could tell he was proud of me, and grateful that I hadn't turned out to be the cripple he thought I'd be. All those times when I thought he didn't care about me, he was probably feeling guilty because he thought he had messed me up for life.

Dad pointed to the bleachers. "Leon's up there waiting for you. Meet us at the car when the fireworks are over."

As I climbed up the bleachers, some of our customers shouted out to tell me I'd pitched a great game.

"Looks like you're the new town hero," Leon said when I got to our spot.

"Big deal," I said. "By tomorrow I'll just be another nobody like you."

Leon grinned at me. "Hey, there's Carl with his grandmother. I'll go see if he wants to sit with us."

As Leon took off, I looked around at the crowd and thought back to last year. When I was lying in that hospital bed, I was sure my life was over. But even though losing my hand was a terrible thing, in some ways it made me try harder. I wondered if the old two-handed Norm would have practiced enough to make the baseball team. Probably not. And he sure wouldn't have been able to pitch the way I did tonight.

I saw Leon coming back up the bleachers without Carl. He reached the top row just in time for the lights to go off and the first rocket to burst over our heads. The boom vibrated my chest like a bass drum.

"Carl says his grandmother can't climb the bleachers, so he'll sit with her," Leon said. "He'll practice with us tomorrow, though. He wants us to work with him, so next time he makes a catch like tonight it's for real and not an accident."

We both laughed about that. Then Leon got serious. "Remember last Fourth of July?"

"You think I could forget it?"

Leon jutted out his chin and looked away from me. "I thought you were going to die."

"You did?"

"Why do you think I rode my bike all the way over to the hospital?" He ducked his head. "I had to see you with my own eyes."

"You wanted to see what I'd look like as a corpse, right?"

Leon grinned and shook his head. "How'd you guess?" A flash of light made his face look orange. "This is what we would have been doing that night—fireworks."

"Except you probably would have blown your hand off lighting them," I said.

"Yeah, probably." There was a big burst of blue sparkles that spread out like stars over the sky. "I don't think I would have done as well with one hand as you have, though. You never gave up, Norm."

"I almost gave up a lot of times."

"Maybe, but you stuck with it, even with me giving you a hard time. I should've helped you more."

"Not really. I needed to figure out a lot of stuff for myself."

"Next time we're up against Brewster, we'll win," Leon said.

"That's for sure. This is going to be the best summer we've ever had." I wasn't just saying that.

I believed it.

AUTHOR'S NOTE

*M*y husband, Herm Auch, lost his left hand while working in his father's meat market as a child. Although this book is a work of fiction, it is loosely based on this childhood accident. Though faced with a personal tragedy at an early age, Herm never let this stop him. He has always said that losing a hand might be the best thing that ever happened to him, because it forced him to think creatively to solve problems. Never considering himself handicapped, Herm learned to excel in a number of sports, even earning a football scholarship for college, which he didn't accept because he wanted to go to art school. He went on to a successful career as a newspaper graphic artist and illustrator. One of Herm's favorite newspaper assignments was riding a bicycle across the entire country with Gannett columnist Dick Dougherty to illustrate a series of stories about how America was settled.

Herm was a tremendous help to me in writing *One-Handed Catch,* describing how he taught himself to play baseball with one hand and other childhood incidents that I could include in Norm's story.

What's true and not true in this book? Norm's accident happens in the same way that Herm's did, but Norm's friends and family members are fictitious characters. Herm's mother, Louise Auch, was similar to Norm's mother in that she made Herm do everything for himself, even though it was painful for her to watch him struggle. She was probably the person most responsible for making Herm believe he could succeed at anything in life.

Go Fish!

GOFISH

MJ AUCH

What did you want to be when you grew up?
A ballerina, an artist, or a veterinarian.

When did you realize you wanted to be a writer?
I had always thought of myself as an artist until I took a weeklong writer's workshop with Natalie Babbitt. When she said she discovered she could paint better pictures with words than paint, that struck a chord with me, and I've been writing ever since.

What was your worst subject in school?
Algebra.

What was your first job?
Designing fabric prints for men's pajamas in the Empire State Building—but only on the fifth floor.

How did you celebrate publishing your first book?
After two years of rejection, I sold my first two novels to two different publishers in the same week. I don't remember any specific celebration, other than being deliriously happy!

Where do you write your books?
I use a laptop, so I can write anywhere. One of my favorite places is on a train, because watching the scenery pass by seems to kick my brain into creative mode. I also like to write on our front porch when weather permits.

Which of your characters is most like you?
There's a little of me in all of my main characters. They all carry my value system and sense of justice.

When you finish a book, who reads it first?
Members of my two critique groups hear the book as I'm writing it. We're lucky to have some wonderful children's writers in our area. Each group meets once a month and we all drive up to an hour to get together. I get valuable early input from writers I respect and trust—Tedd Arnold, Patience Brewster, Bruce Coville, Kathy Coville, Cynthia DeFelice, Alice DeLaCroix, Marsha Hayles, Robin Pulver, and Vivian Vande Velde. The main person I count on is my editor, Christy Ottaviano, who pushes me to take the story far beyond the point I could go alone.

Are you a morning person or a night owl?
I'm a little of each, so I probably don't get enough sleep. I try to write every day when I first wake up, as long as it's after 5 AM. Then I have a tendency to fall asleep watching late-night TV. I guess that makes morning my more productive time.

What's your idea of the best meal ever?
Any meal eaten with good friends.

Which do you like better: cats or dogs?
I was raised with cats as a child, and although I still enjoy them, it has been dogs that have captured my heart. Our last

three dogs have been rescues. It gives me and my husband, Herm, great pleasure to take in a dog that has had a tough life.

What do you value most in your friends?

Two things. First is honesty. I don't like people who play mind games. I like to know straight out what they're thinking. It's hard to have any kind of relationship when people don't tell the truth.

Second but equal is a sense of humor. I admit to being a humor snob. I like people who are spontaneously funny. I'm lucky to have a large group of friends who fall into that category. There is always humor crackling around the room when we get together.

What makes you laugh out loud?

Spontaneous funny conversations with friends. Spending time with genuinely humorous people gives me much more pleasure than so-called professional comedians.

What's your favorite song?

I love playing and singing old jazz standards. Some of my favorites are "Moonlight in Vermont," "A Nightingale Sang in Berkeley Square," and "A Foggy Day in London Town."

What are you most afraid of?

Fire, which was probably what drove me to write *Ashes of Roses*.

What time of the year do you like best?

Fall, especially in the Northeast. It's the one season that doesn't last long enough. I never tire of the reds, golds, and brilliant oranges of the fall foliage.

If you were stranded on a desert island, who would you want for company?
My husband. He's my best friend and soul mate.

If you could travel in time, where would you go?
I'm happy with the years my life has spanned so far. I grew up in simpler times, back in the forties and fifties, and now I get to experience the amazing technological advances we have today. There are many earlier periods that interest me, but I wouldn't want to visit them because of the discomfort factor. They'd be smelly and buggy!

What's the best advice you have ever received about writing?
Don't talk about writing. Just sit down and do it.

What do you want readers to remember about your books?
I hope that they carry the characters with them for a long time and consider them to be friends.

What would you do if you ever stopped writing?
There are lots of other things I enjoy doing. Music is a big part of my life. I love singing three- or four-part harmony. If I weren't a writer, I'd probably be a backup singer. I also enjoy playing string instruments—guitar, banjo, mandolin, and fiddle. I'm not very good at any of these, but I love the challenge of trying to get better.

Other hobbies include designing and sewing clothes. I do this mostly for myself, although I made most of the costumes for our daughter's medieval wedding, and it's fun sewing the costumes for the chickens in our picture books.

I wish I had the time for some serious, non-book-related painting. I was an art major in college, and love doing abstract oils on large canvases.

What do you like best about yourself?
The fact that I'm honest. It gets me in trouble sometimes. I try to be tactful, but I always tell the truth. I think it makes me a friend who can be trusted.

What is your worst habit?
Procrastination. I'd be a lot more productive if I could keep myself from going off on tangents instead of staying focused.

What do you consider to be your greatest accomplishment?
I don't know how much credit I can take for this, but Herm and I raised two wonderful and talented children. They're now both artists in their own right—Kat, a freelance graphic and magazine designer, and Ian, an interactive and motion graphics designer working in advertising. They both have turned into genuinely good human beings.

What do you wish you could do better?
Everything! I love to learn new things, so I'm always working on something—right now it's playing jazz guitar—but I'm always frustrated that I don't progress as fast as I'd like.

What would your readers be most surprised to learn about you?
That I hated history in school. All they had us do was memorize dates of battles. That's why I like to write historical fiction, so I can make a period from the past come to life.

*K*eep reading for an excerpt from
MJ Auch's **Wing Nut,**
available now in paperback from Square Fish.

EXCERPT

Grady Flood couldn't stand the heat of the flames on his face another second. He turned and slipped away from the group that circled the fire. Tonight was the Sunward Path Commune's first bonfire meeting of the year, which Grady knew meant at least a couple hours of boring discussion followed by endless singing. Now that it was April, the weekly meetings could be held outside, which was better than being crowded into the living room of the dilapidated farmhouse. Ever since he turned twelve a few months ago, Grady was considered an adult. He was required to attend meetings, but nobody could force him to listen.

The air was damp with dew as he walked through the darkness up the short driveway to the barn, just far enough away to let his mind wander without getting disapproving looks from the others. Grady settled on a bale of hay and leaned his tired back against the barn wall. He'd spent most of the day transplanting scrawny broccoli plants into the garden. Every muscle in his body ached, which didn't seem fair because he hated broccoli. But then, nothing at Sunward Path was fair.

"Wham! You're dead!" Grady was struck from the side, sending him sprawling on the ground. It was Tran, one of the younger commune boys. Tran was short for Tranquility, which Grady considered the worst case of misnaming a kid he had ever seen.

"I caught the monster," Tran crowed, pummeling Grady on the back. "Die, monster, die!"

Grady twisted around and captured the four-year-old in a hammerlock. "Hey, quiet down, Tran. You want to get us both in trouble?" Grady knew that was an empty threat. The little kids at Sunward Path couldn't get in trouble for anything short of murder, and even then, they'd probably get the benefit of the doubt.

Sunward Path was only one more in a series of dead-end places Grady and Lila had stayed since his father had died seven years ago. Grady had been five at the time. He did the math again in his head to make sure it was right. More than half of his life had been on the move, and the only thing that stayed constant was Lila.

He looked at his mother now, standing among the others. The orange firelight made her long wavy red hair look like it was flame itself. Grady was sure she could be a movie star if they could only make their way out to Hollywood. But Lila had never even tried to get them to California. Instead they had moved around through the Midwest, where she had slaved away at one low-paying job after another. Lila put up with a lot—more than Grady thought she should tolerate—but sooner or later something would get her upset enough to leave, and they'd pack up and take off without having a clue where they were headed.

Grady had a rating system for the places they stayed—ten for the best, one for the worst. Sunward Path was barely a three. They never had stayed at a one or two. A one would mean no food and no bed. Two would be either food or shelter, not both. But since Lila always looked for a job that would give them meals and a place to live, they had never sunk below the level of a three.

Tran wiggled loose from Grady's grip and ran off, but Grady knew he'd be back. There were six kids on the commune, ranging in age from two to seven, and they were pretty much allowed to roam at will. An outsider would have a hard time matching up the six kids with the fifteen adults. Since nobody else seemed to care, Grady had taken it upon himself to make sure none of the little guys got hurt. It wasn't an easy job, especially when he had chores to do. But the kids seemed to sense that Grady cared about them, and he usually had two or three of them following him around as if he were the Pied Piper.

Grady always felt it was his job to protect creatures smaller and more helpless than himself. Didn't matter if they were people or animals. His father had been like that. Anytime somebody found a starving stray dog or an injured wild animal they'd bring it to Arlan Flood. His dad once said he should put up a sign that read "When your car or animal stops running, bring it here. Whatever's broke, we'll fix it."

Grady liked the fact that he had inherited that talent from his father. Arlan Flood had been a big bear of a man, not exactly the kind you'd picture talking in a high little voice while he pulled a splinter from a dog's paw with tweezers, especially since his normal voice sounded more like the blast from an eighteen-wheeler's horn. It always seemed strange to Grady that Lila, who already had a soft, gentle voice, wasn't much good at animal saving. She had such a tender heart, all she ever could do was watch over his dad's shoulder and cry. Not that she was a softie all the time. When she got mad about something, she was like a terrier on a rat.

Grady noticed that the voices around the fire were raised in some sort of an argument, and Lila seemed to be right in the middle of it. He ran back to the group to find out what was going on.

"I can't do this no more," Lila was saying. In the firelight, her cheeks were shiny with tears. "When we first come here, everybody did their share, but now all the cooking and cleaning up falls to me. It's not fair."

Rayden, the commune leader, moved around the circle to put his arm across Lila's shoulders. "Lila, Lila, my dear child. You must understand that things have changed in the months you have been here. We used to be a group of workers, with only one or two philosophers, but now"—his arm gesture swept the circle—"philosophy has become our main focus."

Grady let out a little snort of disgust. Rayden had himself all dressed up to look like Jesus, if you could ignore his nose ring, the snake tattoo winding around his ankle, and the cell phone antenna sticking out of his burlap caftan pocket.

Rayden gave Grady a sharp look, then turned back to Lila. "We count on our group of workers to keep the community functioning to allow the others time for a higher purpose. Of course cooking and washing the dishes is every bit as important as finding the meaning of life, but we each must know our place and accept it." His little speech sounded like he was talking to someone Tran's age. Rayden smiled at the end to show everybody what a good guy he was. What a crock, Grady thought.

Grady heard the sharp intake of air that meant Lila was gearing up to let loose with her temper. Sure enough, Lila pushed Rayden's arm from her shoulders. "You know what, Rayden? You don't have no group of workers. You got me and Grady, and maybe one or two others, who work when the spirit moves them, which isn't very often. Only now you don't even have that, because Grady and me are getting out of here."

Grady squeezed in beside his mother, noticing that his shoulder was only a few inches lower than hers. In spite of the hard work, or maybe because of it, he'd grown a lot in the eight months they'd been here. He wedged himself firmly between Lila and the sweet-talking Rayden. Grady never had trusted that man. Something about Rayden's creepy smile and oily voice made the hairs stand up on the back of his neck. Grady's "crook, cheater, and no-good phony" radar had grown much sharper than his mother's, and he had pegged Rayden for all three right from the beginning.

The other commune members were whispering among themselves now. Tran and his little brother raced around inside the circle, playing tag. Not one of the adults stepped forward to keep the youngsters' bare feet from stepping on the hot coals that had rolled away from the edges of the fire. Grady grabbed the boys as they ran by, then deposited them in front of their mother. "You gotta take care of your kids," he said. "They could get hurt."

The young mother smiled dreamily. "Mother Earth takes care of her own."

"Well, Mother Earth is a lousy babysitter," Grady said, "because I been saving their hides at least a dozen times a day. You gotta watch 'em yerself from now on because I'm not gonna be here. They get in a lot of trouble when they're on their own."

Lila had left the circle and was headed toward the house. Grady ran to catch up, thinking how lucky he was to have a mother who had always looked after him. "You mean it, Mom, right? We're really taking off?"

"Oh, you bet I mean it." Lila's face was red, either from the heat of the fire or from anger. "They can do their high-and-mighty philosophizing all they want, but when their bellies are empty and the garbage and dirty dishes are piled up to the ceiling, maybe they'll wake up." Her voice bumped with each step as she slammed her heels into the ground. "Bunch of no-account snobs. Think they're smart just because their rich daddies sent them to college. I could teach every last one of them a thing or two about common sense."

Grady heard someone coming fast behind them in the dark. It was Russ, the new guy who'd been sniffing around Lila since the day he'd arrived about a month ago. He had come to Sunward Path to do research for a college paper comparing today's communes with the ones from the sixties or some darn fool thing like that. He was somebody else Grady didn't trust, but Lila was usually nice to him. Heck, she was nice to everybody until she saw through them. Russ caught her arm. "Lila, you aren't really thinking of leaving, are you?"

"Just watch me." Lila didn't break her stride.

"But where will you go?"

"Who knows? Anything's better than here."

ALSO AVAILABLE
FROM SQUARE FISH BOOKS

If you like sports, you'll love these SQUARE FISH sports books!

Airball • L. D. Harkrader
ISBN-13: 978-0-312-37382-5 • $6.99 U.S./$7.99 Can.
"Even non-basketball fans will savor the on-court action and will cheer loudly for these determined players." —*Publishers Weekly*

Busted! • Betty Hicks
ISBN-13: 978-0-312-38053-3 • $6.99 U.S./$7.99 Can.
"Soccer fans will appreciate the exciting game action....A winning combination of sports and humor." —*School Library Journal*

Getting in the Game • Dawn FitzGerald
ISBN-13: 978-0-312-37753-3 • $6.99 U.S./$8.99 Can.
"Fast and funny...and readers who are caught up by the sports will stay around for the family and friendship drama." —*Booklist*

Soccer Chick Rules • Dawn FitzGerald
ISBN-13: 978-0-312-37662-8 • $6.99 U.S./$8.99 Can.
"An expression of the sheer joy of athletic competition and the hard-breathing fray of the game." —*Kirkus Reviews*

SQUARE FISH
WWW.SQUAREFISHBOOKS.COM
AVAILABLE WHEREVER BOOKS ARE SOLD